"So, old friends, huh?"

Scott grew silent and rested his forearms on his knees.

"Seemed like th[...] a glance in his di[...] e intensity in his e[...]

"You were a hel[...] o me," he said, an[...]

If she was so much more of a friend to him, then why did he leave without a trace?

There you go again, Emily scolded herself. The past was over. What was done was done. When her father died, she had learned to savor the moment, to not take the present for granted. Sometimes it was easy to lose sight of that, especially more recently, when she was too busy getting lost in the future and all of its conflicting possibilities.

She straightened her shoulders. There would be no thinking about the future today. Today was all anyone really had.

A little shiver down her spine told her that today she had everything she had ever wanted, anyway.

Dear Reader,

Some of my fondest memories are those spent in the kitchen, gathered around the table for a family meal. I've always seen food as a way to bring people together, to give them a shared experience, and an opportunity to slow down and savor a moment. I collect cookbooks of all kinds (often to simply admire the beautiful photos, though I make a point of buying each of Martha Stewart's books), but the most special recipes I have in my repertoire are the ones that have been passed down.

For as long as I can remember, my mother has used a single cookbook: *Joy of Cooking.* It's old and worn, with a loose spine and yellowed pages, and within its pages are the recipes I enjoyed as a child, on days when chicken pot pie could ease a broken heart or an apple pie with cinnamon crust could define a holiday. Not a birthday went by that I didn't request Thanksgiving dinner...in March! The cookbook is stuffed with scraps of paper in all shapes and sizes, handwritten recipes jotted down in fading ink in a familiar scrawl—handwriting that is as eternally comforting as a slice of warm pie on a cold day.

In writing *Recipe for Romance,* I wanted to evoke a sense of nostalgia for the characters, and an overall feeling of coming home. Setting much of this story in a pie shop, where Emily could keep her family's tradition alive, underscored everything that Emily ever represented to Scott, and everything that had been missing from his life since he left Maple Woods: family, togetherness and memories meant to be cherished.

One of my favorite scenes in this book was when Emily and Scott shared a pie made from a much loved recipe and turned a corner in their relationship. I'd like to think it signifies that no matter where you are, or how many years have passed, the taste and smell of a familiar recipe have the power to bring you home again.

Best wishes,

Olivia

Recipe for Romance

—

Olivia Miles

HARLEQUIN® SPECIAL EDITION®

Recycling programs
for this product may
not exist in your area.

ISBN-13: 978-0-373-65810-7

RECIPE FOR ROMANCE

Copyright © 2014 by Megan Leavell

Printed in U.S.A.

For my family,
for their love, support, and encouragement.

And for my editor, Susan Litman,
for her invaluable feedback and guidance.

Chapter One

Reaching behind her waist to tie the strings of her crisp cotton apron in a jaunty bow, Emily Porter kept a firm eye on the clock, waiting with a quickening of her pulse until the long hand finally ticked to the twelve. She glanced to her friend and boss, Lucy Miller, who gave a nervous smile followed by a simple nod of her head. Eleven o'clock. This was it!

With a deep breath, Emily crossed the polished wood floors and turned the homemade sign on the door of the Sweetie Pie Bakery. They were officially open for business.

"I haven't been this nervous since my wedding day," Lucy exclaimed giddily, her voice high with sudden emotion.

"It'll be a huge success. I just know it," Emily said, grinning ear to ear. This was the most exciting day she'd had in a long time, and heck, it hadn't even started yet! Her stomach fluttered with anticipation as she glanced around the sun-filled bakery. The past few weeks had flown by in such a whirlwind of activity to get everything ready for the opening day that she hadn't stopped to stand back and take it all in. The walls were painted a creamy ivory, nearly the same shade as the sleek cabinets that lined the wall behind the gleaming glass display case now housing fifteen different kinds of pie, all baked fresh that morning, with more in stock in the kitchen. The counter was a warm rustic cherrywood, chosen to complement the spotless floor. Ten cozy tables dotted the room, all eagerly awaiting the guests who would soon be coming through the front door.

"I hope so." Lucy sighed, glancing out the wall of windows onto Main Street.

It was the first time Emily had seen her friend express any doubts since she'd first announced she was going through with the venture. She'd been working for Lucy for as long as she could remember at the diner across the street and never in all that time had she seen her boss so flustered.

"You've been in the restaurant business for almost twenty years," Emily replied, coming around the counter to get the coffee started.

"You calling me old?" Lucy winked. Then, on a sigh, she admitted, "You're right…" She began straightening chairs that were already straight. "I just don't want to let anyone down."

Emily poured another heaping spoonful of fresh coffee grounds into the filter. "You aren't going to let anyone down. Everyone in Maple Woods loves your diner and there's no reason why they won't love this place, too."

Lucy brushed an imaginary crumb from her pink and white pinstriped apron and squared her shoulders. "What would I do without you, Em?"

A ripple of guilt crept over Emily, but she pushed the feeling aside as quickly as it formed and distracted herself by setting the coffee to brew. She glanced around the bakery once more, wishing someone would just come in already! Deciding there was nothing left to do but wait until the first customer made their appearance, she announced, "I'll water the flower beds."

Lucy nodded her approval, her eyes never leaving the window.

"You know what they say about a watched pot..." Emily teased as she pushed through the front door with a wide grin, feeling the warmth of late morning sunshine on her arms and face.

Bright pink tulips lined the tall windows of the storefront, and Emily gave each one a healthy drink while gazing down Main Street, which was unusually quiet for this time of day. In an hour the lunch crowd would hit, and then...then Emily didn't know what to expect. She had visions of people pushing through a crammed door, eager to take a peek inside Maple Woods's newest establishment.

Still smiling at the thought, she whipped around to the sound of an engine revving in the near distance. A bright red sports car was sitting at the intersection of Main Street and Maple Avenue, the noise a dramatic contrast to the peaceful and simple life of Maple Woods.

Emily watched as the car took a sharp left when

the light turned, wincing as the vehicle rumbled offensively and took speed in her direction. She squinted into the sunlight as it quickly closed the distance, but as it zipped past her, her eyes shot open.

It couldn't be...not *him.* After all these years, there was no way. Why now?

Emily peered at the sidewalk as she tried to logically process what she had just seen. Her stomach tightened with each ragged breath. Scott Collins hadn't shown his face in this town in nearly twelve years. Would he really come back now, after all this time?

She pursed her lips. It had taken months of heartache and waiting to learn the answer to that question. It was about time she accepted it, too.

She swallowed the knot of disappointment that was quickly forming a lump in her throat, replacing her sudden shock. She hadn't thought of her high school sweetheart in years, and look at her: all it took was one drive-by, one trigger to open wounds she thought had finally healed. One double take to have her thinking of those blue eyes and that lopsided grin all over again.

She shook her head and pulled open the door to the bakery. The car had been too fast. Her mind had been playing tricks on her. Besides, Lucy would have surely announced if her own brother was paying a visit.

"I just got a call from George," Lucy announced breathlessly as soon as the door closed behind Emily. She finished untying the strings to her apron and hung it on a hook on the back of the kitchen door. "He needs me at the diner for a bit to help prep for the lunch crowd, seeing that we don't have any customers here yet." The last words of her statement were laced with disappointment.

Emily studied Lucy's face thoughtfully, wondering if she should even mention her possible sighting, but her friend's expression showed nothing that would indicate Scott's arrival any more than her words did.

"Hurry back if you can," Emily said as Lucy gathered her things to hurry to the diner that she owned with her husband. "I have a feeling that by tonight, we'll be so busy, we'll be wishing everyone would just go home." She paused to stare out the window, idly searching for the mysterious red car. Suspicion engulfed her all over again. No one in Maple Woods drove a car like that. She turned back to Lucy. "Were you expecting anyone special for today's grand opening?"

She knew from Lucy that her father wasn't well… but no. Scott hadn't so much as bothered to come back for a holiday in all these years. Surely he wasn't suddenly sweeping into town looking to make up for lost time. Unless…

"Just the usual group of friends and family showing their support." Lucy shrugged. She surveyed the empty room once more, her lips thinning. "I'm off, then. Call if you need me. I'll just be across the street."

"Will do," Emily said, sighing. *Silly girl,* she thought with a shake of her head. Of course it hadn't been Scott. He was gone, never coming back.

Besides, she was better off without him.

What the hell was he doing here?

Scott leaned on the hood of the red Porsche, his eyes narrowing as his gaze swept down Main Street

and over to the town square. The charming little gazebo bordered with hydrangea bushes. The bronze
statue of the town's founder standing tall and proud
under the umbrella of a magnolia tree. His stare lingered on Lucy's Place, his gut knotting at the familiar
sight. In all his life, he never expected to see that diner
again, or any place in Maple Woods, really. There
was no circumstance that could bring him back, he'd
thought, and yet here he was.

He shook his head in disgust, angry at himself for
giving in. He shouldn't have come back. He should
have stayed away. Twelve years was a long time. Longer than the innocence of some childhoods. Longer
than most marriages. But twelve years wasn't enough
time to put distance between him and Maple Woods.
Or the secret the town held. The one he had sworn he
would take to his grave.

Scott turned and regarded his rental car, grimacing
with regret. He'd rented the exact model he owned in
Seattle, out of habit, but with its flashy red paint and
six-figure price tag, that car didn't belong in Maple
Woods any more than he did. It would only garner
more unwanted attention and speculation, and God
knew this town was full of enough gossip. Sleepy little towns like this enjoyed a good scandal, or in his
case, a good secret. It kept things interesting, and gave
an otherwise dormant community something to talk
about other than marriages and births. Deaths.

Scott scowled as his stomach began to burn again.
It had been happening a lot lately—ever since Lucy
had called and begged him to come back to Maple
Woods, pleading with him to take over the rebuilding
of the town library, which her son had damaged in a

fire he had accidentally started. "Kids," Scott had told her over the phone, when she'd tearfully explained his nephew's involvement, but something about it touched a nerve, evoking memories that were better kept buried. Lucy wanted to set things right: Bobby was doing community service, he was working hard to get into a good college on a football scholarship, and the plans for the new library were moving along nicely...until their father got sick.

He didn't know why he gave in to her request in the end. Maybe it was because she'd let him stay away as long as she had, maybe it was because he respected her need to set things right for the wrongdoings of her son, or maybe it was because she didn't ask him directly to come back and be there for the family in their hour of need that he felt he couldn't say no to her. Whatever the reason, he was here.

You're gonna pay me back for this one, Lucy.

His breath hitched on a rueful laugh. Who was he kidding? He could never stay mad at her for long. How could he? With their seven-year age difference, they'd never had the kind of banter or rivalry one expects with siblings. Lucy had always doted on him, right up until the time she married George Miller and moved across town to start a family of her own.

She would probably be in the diner right now, filling coffee mugs with that no-nonsense grin and a twinkle in her eye. In a matter of minutes he could see her again. He had to admit the idea of it was appealing, despite the circumstances.

Scott pushed back from the car and straightened his shoulders. Hands thrust into his pockets, he began wandering down the sidewalk, taking his time in surveying the shops that lined the quaint street. He was struck with wonder as his eyes roamed over the storefronts. Absolutely nothing had changed. It was all the same. The pizza place. The flower shop. The bookstore. The fashions in the window of the clothing boutique sure had changed, though. He paused to study the dress on the mannequin with furrowed interest before his gaze slid to a wide-eyed face staring back at him through the glass. He flushed as the woman mouthed what he was nearly sure was "Oh, my *God,* it's Scott *Collins!*" and another slack-jawed face quickly appeared on the other side of the mannequin, eyes gleaming in the ray of sunlight that poured through the shop window.

Scott frowned before turning on his heel and quickening his pace toward the diner. He remembered those girls, all right. Women now. They were both in his math class senior year. They'd been some of the prettiest girls on the cheerleading squad. From the looks of it, they'd remembered him, too.

He'd put a hundred bucks on the notion that the women in the clothing shop were calling around to every one of their old classmates right this moment and grimaced to think of the reaction he was going to elicit when he pushed through the doors of Lucy's Place. After all, a man didn't disappear from this town for twelve years without prompting a reaction when he returned.

He didn't think he could stomach it, honestly.

Scott closed his eyes as his chest tightened. He could only hope that one person could be spared. If he was in and out of town quick enough, he might manage to avoid her altogether.

A chalkboard sign up ahead boasted the loopy
script Grand Opening! and Scott grinned. Of course!
Lucy's new bakery. She had mentioned on the phone
that she was planning to launch this week but his mind
had been so muddled with the thought of his return
that he'd almost forgotten. He glanced to the diner
across the street, noting the swarm of customers filling every table near the windows and exhaled in relief.

He couldn't face that diner—those curious faces
and eager smiles—and now he wouldn't have to. He
strode up to the bakery and registered the open sign.
One glance through the windows revealed an empty
establishment: a safe haven. With any luck he'd have
a chance to catch his breath and reunite with his sister
without forty sets of eyes memorizing the exchange,
eager to report it verbatim at the dinner table later
that evening.

He glanced back up the street to where the women
from the clothing shop were now standing on the sidewalk, cell phones pressed against their ears, staring at
him as if he was some carnival freak. He swallowed
the acidic taste that filled his mouth.

It had been a bad idea to come back here. He had
known it would be difficult to face his past but he
hadn't realized how quickly the emotions he had tried
to bury would bubble to the surface. Well, all the more
reason to do his business and then get the hell out.
And this time, he wouldn't be back. Under any circumstances.

The bells above the front door chimed, causing
Emily to jump. The cookbook she'd been holding slid
to the cool marble kitchen island with a thud. Their

first official customer. Nearly an hour had passed since they'd opened, and she'd just managed to relax. Now butterflies danced through her stomach as Emily quickly smoothed her apron and made her way out of the kitchen and into the cheerful storefront.

"Welcome to Sweetie Pie! What can I—" She halted abruptly, her voice locking in her throat.

Scott Collins stood before the display case, casually eyeing the selection. His hands were pushed deep into the pockets of his chinos, accentuating his broad chest and well-toned arms. It had been twelve years since she'd seen him, standing in the glow of the summer sunset, waving to her from the base of her peeling front stoop, that lopsided grin tugging at her heart as she turned her back and retreated into the shadows of her old farmhouse—but she had been wrong in thinking she wouldn't recognize him now. He was just as handsome as he had ever been. Even more so, as luck would have it.

He lifted his sparkling blue eyes to her now, his lips already curling, causing her heart to flutter in a way she didn't think it could anymore. His ash-brown hair was cut in a more conservative style than she remembered, and he'd bulked up in all the right places, but one thing hadn't changed. He still had a smile that could stop traffic. And make her heart skip a beat.

Twelve years later and he still had this effect on her. *Damn him.*

But as his eyes met hers, his expression froze. That irresistible grin faltered.

"Emily." His voice was gruff.

"Scott." His name felt unnatural on her tongue. "What a surprise." *The understatement of a decade.*

"I didn't know you worked here," Scott said. "I mean...I didn't expect to see you. Lucy hadn't told me... This, well... It's nice to see you," he settled on.

Emily narrowed her gaze as he stumbled over his words, trying to draw some explanation from him, something that would clarify what had happened all those years ago. What had gone wrong? What had caused him to leave town without a word, without any hint or preparation, to break her heart and all his promises in one fell swoop?

Her heart squeezed as his turquoise gaze sliced right through her. "I didn't expect to see you around here again," she said. When he didn't respond, she added, "I just started working here, actually." She brushed aside the twinge of hurt that Lucy hadn't mentioned it to him. That she meant so little. That she was so forgotten. "Today's our grand opening, but I'm sure Lucy mentioned that to you."

"Is she here?" Scott looked hopefully around the empty room.

Emily shook her head. "She's at the diner, but she'll be back soon. Funny, she didn't tell me you'd be stopping by."

Scott grinned nervously. "She probably didn't want to jinx it. I don't exactly have the best track record for homecomings."

Emily's brows inadvertently pinched. She studied him for a long moment, gathering her thoughts, forcing a deep breath to temper her racing pulse.

"So, how've you been?" she asked, bracing herself for the answer. Lucy barely mentioned Scott, and no one else in town kept in touch with him. When Scott left home, he'd severed all ties. With his family, his friends. With her.

"Good enough," Scott said with a shrug. He dropped his gaze. He couldn't even look her in the eye.
Coward.

"Where are you living these days?" she tried again, disappointment tugging at her that two people who had once known every inch of each other, who finished each other's sentences, who shared the same dreams, could be reduced to this sort of awkward conversation. They were strangers now.

"Seattle," he replied, and Emily frowned. She knew he had gone to college in Chicago and had just assumed he'd stayed there. But all this time he had been living in Seattle, and for some reason that depressed the hell out of her.

She paused. "Married? Kids?" she asked, because there was no point in holding back. After all, she'd lost him a long time ago.

"Nope," he said, and in spite of herself, Emily felt her shoulders relax. "So you're still in town," he observed.

She gazed at him, disarmed by the incongruity between his sudden reappearance and the nonchalant way he strode into town. Nothing fazed the man—not then and, it would seem, not now. Silence stretched between them; the only sound audible was the pounding of her own heart and God did she hope he couldn't hear it, too.

"Yep." Emily she said tightly. "Never left." Twelve years after Scott had disappeared from Maple Woods, she was still right where he had left her. *Pathetic.*

Scott nodded again, dropping his gaze to the floor

as his face reddened, and she knew she had hit a nerve. Well, good! It was about time that Scott gave some sort of reaction for what he had done to her, even if it was a decade or so too late.

"I always wondered about that," he said, his voice so low she had to strain to hear. "I always wondered about you," he said, looking up to properly meet her eyes.

Emily's stomach rolled over, but she pushed back the temptation to dwell on his words, to extract more meaning from them than he'd probably intended. She straightened her spine.

"Well, you could have called. Or written." She cursed herself for allowing the hurt to creep into her voice. But damn it, she couldn't help it! His words were empty, falling flat and meaningless. She wondered briefly how many of the other things he had said to her were equally insincere. Most of them, she decided. As much as she hated to realize this, it was just the cold hard truth.

"I've never been good about keeping in touch. No matter how much I wanted to be," Scott said, frowning. His eyes locked with hers until her pulse skipped and she had to look away.

He wasn't here for her. He hadn't come back for her. That was all that mattered.

"I'm sure Lucy's eager to see you," she blurted. "Half the town is at the diner for lunch. I'm sure they'd be thrilled to see you walk in." Scott was the high school football star, after all, the kid from the good family with the good looks and "things going for him." He had always been loved around town. Especially by her.

"I had hoped to avoid the diner for a while," he admitted, offering her a rueful grin. "At least until everyone knows I'm back in town."

"People do love to talk around here," she mused as she set a stack of napkins next to the cash register.

Their gazes locked and she noted the warmth of his smoky blue eyes, and felt nearly sick with humiliation at the pity she saw float through them. She didn't want his sympathy, or anyone else's for that matter. She wanted to break free, to start over. To live a life where she could be so many more things than this town had allowed her to be.

"Too much," Scott said quickly, and Emily gave him a brief, tight smile. He knew the things people used to say about her family. It hung in the air, in the leaves of the maple trees that lined Main Street. It triggered family dinner conversations and prompted Sunday prayers. It was a name spoken in whisper, with lowered eyes and a shake of the head. *Those poor Porters.*

Emily shook herself from the darkening thoughts. "Well, I've just put on some fresh coffee and there's plenty of pie. Feel free to wait here, if you'd like."

He hesitated, shifting back on his heels. "Why not?" he suddenly said with a shrug. His eyes softened their hold on hers, causing her pulse to skip a beat.

"How about a slice of pie?" she asked nervously, squeezing her fists to keep her hands from shaking. "There's strawberry and cream, pecan, apple crumb—oh, we have a lovely cherry here," she offered before she could stop herself. She hadn't even remembered until now that it was his favorite.

"You know me well," he said with a sigh, sliding into a seat at the counter.

Emily offered him a small smile in return, then, her heart heavy, turned her back to him to plate the pie, paying careful attention in getting the first wedge just right. It was tricky, but she'd learned the knack through practice. Long before her father had died on a construction site when she was just a little girl, Sunday pie had been a ritual in her household, and she still took comfort in his memory every time she pulled one from the oven. No matter how rough the week had been, there was always some reassurance in the time-honored tradition. Pie could bring comfort in a world that could be cruel. It was something to be shared. It brought people together. In the most difficult of circumstances, she liked to think it helped keep them together, too.

"Here you go," she said to Scott now. "I made it this morning, so it's fresh."

"You always made the best pies, Emily Porter." He grinned, and his eyes shone bright on hers until he caught the heat in her expression and looked down at his plate.

She sucked in a breath. "So," she said briskly. "What brings you back to town?" It certainly wasn't her. He'd made a promise—dozens of beautiful, hope-filled promises—and broken each one right along with her heart.

"My dad asked me to help oversee the construction of the library." His jaw twitched and he scratched at a day's worth of stubble. "Well, Lucy asked, actually."

"Lucy mentioned once that you were in construction, just like you'd always planned." She frowned at the thought. Why couldn't he have stayed in Maple Woods and taken over Collins Construction, the family business? It was a fine company, well respected by the town. Her own father had proudly worked there.

Scott paused. "My father isn't up to the job at the moment."

Emily nodded. Scott and Lucy's parents had never been warm to her, but she'd decided a long time ago not to take it personally. Her father had worked for Mr. Collins for more than fifteen years before the accident on the job took his life when she was eight years old. It had been human error, the police had said, his own negligence in failing to put the emergency brakes on the excavator that rolled down the slope and killed him. Mr. Collins had been there that day. He'd dealt with the police, and as a courtesy to the family he had helped cover the funeral expenses, but he had been tense around her family in passing ever since.

"Sticking around for long?" She held her breath, waiting for an answer she knew deep down wouldn't make a lick of difference.

"Only as long as I have to."

Emily held his sharp gaze and then lowered her eyes with a slow nod of her head as her heart began to tug. He was still the same old Scott. The same charming guy with dreams beyond Maple Woods. And she was still the same old Emily, still living in the same small town, still waiting for life to really start.

Well, it was time to do something about that.

Of all the people he had hoped to avoid in this town, Emily was at the top of his list. So he supposed it made sense that she was the first person he ran into. The one girl who had crawled under his skin and remained there. No matter how much he wanted to resist her, to turn his back and leave, he just couldn't.

He rested an elbow on the counter, grateful for its barrier. If it wasn't there, keeping them apart, he wasn't quite sure he would have been able to refrain himself from greeting her with a hug, to feel the warmth of her body pressed against his, to hold her close and know that she was real and that she was okay. That no matter what had happened, what he had done, that she was all right.

It wasn't supposed to be this way with them. They'd had plans—plans he'd intended to stick to—until that horrible summer night, his last night in this town, when his entire world came crashing down around him and Emily was lost to him forever.

Swallowing hard, he allowed his gaze to roam over her as she repositioned the pie plate on its stand and swept some crumbs off the counter, her glossy chestnut waves cascading over her shoulders. He couldn't peel his eyes from her. His high school sweetheart— the girl who interrupted his dreams and haunted his waking hours was standing right in front of him, looking more beautiful than ever.

But time hadn't changed one thing. Emily was still off-limits.

"So what have you been up to all this time?" he asked, even though he didn't want to hear it confirmed. Emily had always had dreams. Dreams beyond this small town. Dreams that hadn't come true.

"Oh, not much," she said. "I worked at the diner before this, but you might have known that."

His stomach twisted at her words. Emily was the

smartest girl he'd known back in school. She should be running a restaurant of her own, not waiting tables. She should have gone to college, pursued her passions—opportunities she would have had if her father had lived. If his father hadn't deprived their family of insurance money that was rightfully owed to them as a result of the tragic accident. If Scott hadn't been on that construction site at all the day that Mr. Porter...

"No," he managed. "No, Lucy hadn't mentioned it."

Her eyes narrowed ever so slightly, before she pulled back and leaned against the far counter, crossing her arms over her chest. "Ah, well, I suppose you and Lucy have better things to talk about than some girl you used to know."

The hurt in her tone sliced through him, but the pain in her eyes was his true punishment. He'd earned it. He'd deserved it. He'd take it.

"You were more than some girl, Em."

She lifted her eyes to his, holding his stare for a beat, and then shrugged.

"Well." He sighed, "I should probably brace myself for the gossip mill." He gave a tight smile and set his fork on the edge of the empty plate. "If Lucy knew I was already in town and hadn't come to see her yet, she'd probably never forgive me."

"Probably for the best," Emily said softly. "It looks busy over there today. I won't be surprised if she's kept longer than she wants to be."

Scott stood and reached into his pocket for his wallet but Emily frowned and held up her hand. "No, please. It's on the house."

"Oh, come on," he said, frowning. *Take the money,*

Emily. Take what is owed you, what you should have had a long time ago. Take what my family stole from you. "It's your opening day. I want to help."

But Emily was adamant, shaking her head. "Lucy would never forgive me," she insisted, falling back on his own words, and he knew she had him there.

"I guess I'll get going then," he said, but he didn't move toward the door. For twelve years he had done nothing but imagine this moment, the things he would say to her if he ever saw her again. But he couldn't say them. And that was why he had never come back.

"Bye, Scott," she said coolly.

He gave a tight smile. "Bye, Em." He turned and walked to the door, pushed through it out into the warm glow of the morning sun and crossed the street, focused on the diner in front of him growing nearer with each step, his heart thudding in his chest.

He knew this feeling. It was the same one he'd had when he'd packed up his bags and gotten into his car that late-summer night twelve years ago after he'd overheard his parents talking about Richard Porter's death—after he'd found out what he had done, what they had covered up for nine years, only revealing the details once it was too late, once he was already in love with Emily, once he was eighteen and old enough to feel the toll of his actions, however unintentional. He'd sped out of town before he had a chance to look back, to think of what he was leaving behind, his heart breaking as he swore he would never love again.

He didn't deserve love.

And he certainly didn't deserve Emily.

There was no amount of time or distance that could put Emily Porter behind him. Oh, he'd tried all right.

He'd gone to the far end of the country, putting as many miles between him and Maple Woods as possible, only his dark, dirty secret to keep him company and serve as an aching memory of everyone he'd left behind. Of why he could never return.

He was the reason Emily had grown up without a father. He was the reason she'd been stuck in the mercy of this town and all its limitations, and that wasn't something he could ever forget. But it was something he would have to set right. Once and for all.

Chapter Two

The steady trill of the alarm clock pulled Emily from a deep slumber. She blindly slapped at it and rolled over in bed. The grand opening of Sweetie Pie had kept her at work longer than she'd expected, plus she'd stayed late to prep for today. Poor Lucy had been so busy bouncing from the diner to the bakery that she had barely stopped to take a breath. They hadn't even had a moment to discuss Scott's return.

Scott. At the memory of his startling arrival the day before, Emily's eyes popped open, and she sprang out of bed. She showered and dressed quickly, quietly, so as not to wake her sister Julia, who rarely emerged from her bed before eight. Tiptoeing through the living room, she paused at the stack of yesterday's mail piled neatly on the small table just beside the front door. She had been so preoccupied with seeing Scott again that she had failed to check the mailbox on her way home last night. It wasn't like her, and with a frown she realized the hold he still had over her nearly a dozen years later.

Recalling his words yesterday, she shook her head and silently scolded herself. She'd been a fool to pin any hopes on that man. There was nothing in Maple Woods for Scott—there never had been, it seemed—and he made it very clear that he wasn't planning on staying in town for long.

Well, neither am I.

Her heart began to thump as she picked up the stack of crisp envelopes and began thumbing through them. When she reached the end, she sighed—possibly in relief, possibly in disappointment. She wasn't sure which anymore. It had been three months since she'd sent her application to the cooking school in Boston, and as the weeks passed without a response, her anxiety grew stronger. So many hopes were hitched to this opportunity that a part of her was happy her fate wasn't yet sealed. It was good to have a dream, and this had been hers for as long as she could remember. She wasn't ready for it to be over just yet.

The bakery still wouldn't be open for another two hours, but the day was still young and there was plenty of work to do. Lucy was a pie-making expert—there was no denying her skill—but when she'd tasted a few of Emily's creations, she had decided to feature those each day, as well. Emily had free rein on what she could create.

Emily gave a sad smile whenever she thought of the irony of the situation—who would have known she'd get such an opportunity just when she might be able to finally break free of this town once and for all?

Determined to think about nothing but the second day at Sweetie Pie, she rolled up her sleeves and went into the kitchen. A couple hours of straight-up baking, fortified by strong coffee, were sure to banish the blues that had set in when Scott walked through that door yesterday.

"Oh, thank goodness you're up!" Julia gushed, bursting into the kitchen half an hour later, already dressed for her job at the yarn shop. Her cheeks were flushed and her green eyes flashed with excitement as she quickly pulled her hair into a ponytail.

"Good morning to you, too," Emily said mildly as she finished slicing pears into a bowl and showered them with sugar.

Julia's eyes danced. "You will *never* believe who is back in town!"

Emily smiled as she measured out a cup of flour, then diced a stick of cold butter and pulsed the mixture in the food processor with a teaspoon each of sugar and salt. This was a little game of theirs, and even at their age, it was endlessly amusing, adding a bit of suspense to an otherwise routine life. Julia would come home with a juicy bit of gossip, usually about who was dating whom, and question by question, Emily would narrow it down until the titillating conclusion was reached. Sadly, on this occasion, there was no buildup of clues; Emily already knew the answer.

"Scott Collins," she said and immediately wished she had just played along when she saw Julia's face fall with disappointment.

"You knew?" she cried. "And here I nearly shook you awake last night to tell you!"

"He came into the bakery yesterday," Emily said.

"Did you speak to him?" Julia's eyes were wide with interest. "What was he like?"

Emily heaved a sigh. "Not much different than I remembered," she admitted, catching the wistful edge to her tone.

"Still a hunk then, huh?" Julia dipped her finger into the sugar canister, and Emily rolled her eyes.

"Still a hunk, as you so delicately put it."

Julia regarded her for a long moment, a dreamy look creeping over her face, as if she were lost in time, clinging to a memory. "Sorry," she said, straightening herself. "I know it's a touchy subject."

"I was seventeen," Emily reminded her. "It didn't mean anything." *Clearly.*

"Well, it meant something to me." Julia lifted her chin, her eyes suddenly darkening at the memory. "I still haven't forgotten the way he took off without so much as a goodbye."

"Really?" Emily narrowed her gaze in mock confusion. "Because you seemed to have completely forgotten about that episode when you came bounding in here two minutes ago." She flashed her sister a rueful grin as she formed the dough into a disk and wrapped it in cellophane. She set it in the fridge to chill, swapping it for one that had cooled, and plucked her rolling pin from the drawer beneath the stove.

"Well, I admit, I did get a little swept up in the memory of how handsome he was," Julia explained, and Emily bit her lip to keep from laughing. "But the truth is that he treated you like a first-rate jerk, leaving you like that, without any explanation."

They were supposed to have gone to a movie the next night. Emily could still remember sitting on the steps of her front porch, waiting. She'd called his house, worried he might be sick or worse—that he'd had an accident. It was a fear of hers ever since she was little, since her father had died. Instead she was told in clipped tones by Scott's father that he was gone. He'd left town the night before, and they didn't know when he'd be back. *If* he'd be back. And he never did come back. Until now.

Emily shrugged off the twinge of hurt with a smile. "Please, Julia. That was ancient history. We were kids."

Julia watched her carefully. "If you say so."

"Are you accusing me of still pining after Scott Collins?"

Julia tipped her head. "I just thought that you would be interested to know he was back in town. That's all." She paused. "So…is he married?"

"No," Emily said, stirring more forcefully.

"And you know this—"

"Because he told me," Emily huffed, whipping around to face her sister. "Because I asked, okay. I… asked." It was a normal question, she told herself, but probably not when it was posed to the man whom she had once imagined an entire future with. His answer had filled her with a surge of hope that had no business being there.

A spark passed through Julia's bright green eyes. "Huh. Interesting."

"What's that supposed to mean?"

"Nothing." Julia shrugged. "Nothing at all." She smiled conspiratorially and then breezed out the door, as if there was nothing left of the subject to discuss.

Emily shook her head and chuckled softly. Leave it to her sister to get carried away with Scott's reemergence and the impact it might have on her. Of course she was interested to know that Scott was back. More interested than she should be. And that was just the problem.

Before she left the house, Emily took extra care in brushing her hair and selecting just the right shade of lipstick. It was silly, she knew, and she was probably jinxing herself with the effort, but if there was a chance of seeing Scott again today, she wanted to be ready.

Let him see what he's been missing.

"Well, don't you look pretty today!" Lucy proclaimed as Emily pushed through the back door of the bakery into the kitchen.

Emily shrugged off the compliment with a wry grin and tied an apron around her waist. "What's the plan for day two?"

Lucy regarded her suspiciously for a lingering moment and then, with a lift of her brow, changed the subject. Emily made a mental note to swipe off her lipstick the first chance she had. She felt suddenly self-conscious and foolish and overly aware of herself. She had never liked being the center of attention, and here she was, trying to be front and center in Scott's mind.

"Mayor Pearson agreed to the pie toss," Lucy said, and Emily smiled. Flyers and word of mouth went far in a small town such as this, but a little promotion helped with a new business, too. "I'm hoping it will pull in more customers today."

"I'm sure it will help get the word out." Emily thought of how the mayor prided himself on Maple Woods's sense of community. "People might love him, but I doubt few would resist the chance to see him covered in whipped cream."

"I'm hoping so." Lucy studied her inventory list. "A fresh shipment of apricots arrived this morning, so let's use those up where we can."

Emily carefully removed the three pies she had baked that morning from their boxes. "I made a pear-and-cherry tart this morning." She began plating it for display. "I'll start prepping a few apricot pies next. A lattice crust would be nice for those, don't you think?"

"What would I do without you?" Lucy said on a sigh of content.

Emily lowered her head, unable to answer the question knowing the information she was withholding, and pulled a canister of flour off the shelf, waiting for the wave of guilt to subside. She was getting ahead of herself, she finally reasoned. There was nothing to feel bad about yet. She might not even get into that school in Boston. There was no use getting worked up over something that might never even happen.

Feeling slightly better, she went about her task as Lucy brewed coffee, the pair working in companionable silence for a while until Emily finally dared to observe, "So…Scott's back in town."

Lucy whipped around. "Can you believe it?"

Emily opened her eyes wide. "Not really." She forced back the image of his handsome face by gathering ingredients from the refrigerator. "You must be really happy," she managed, hoping Lucy didn't detect the note of hurt that laced her words. She couldn't help it. She still wasn't over it. Twelve years later and that man still hadn't explained himself! Was he so beyond reproach?

She winced. He probably didn't think she cared anymore. After all, he obviously didn't.

Lucy huffed out a breath. "Yesterday was quite a day. The opening of this place, then seeing Scott again…" She paused. "I had to really work on him to come back here at all and a part of me still didn't think he really would—I guess I didn't dare to believe it until I finally saw him."

"It's been a long time." Emily nodded in understanding.

"Too long. When he first left town, I kept hoping he would be back one day. Then I guess I just learned to give up on that hope."

Emily looked down. *That made two of us.*

Her heart began to ache in that all too familiar way as she washed the apricots and set them to dry. It was the same feeling she got every time she thought of Scott over the years. Why did he have to come back? Why couldn't he have just stayed away forever? Surely at some point she would have forgotten the way his grin could make her heart skip a beat, or the way her hair rustled when he whispered in her ear. A dozen years might not have done the trick, but a dozen more might have…

She watched Lucy silently, wondering if she would say more, but Lucy just tied her apron strings, grabbed two pies, and tapped her hip against the swinging kitchen door. Emily sighed and got to work herself. She had always wondered why Scott had stayed away, but it wasn't her place to ask Lucy. Anyone who avoided Maple Woods for a dozen years had a reason. A big one.

Her heart dropped as she pulled out the cutting board. If Scott was that determined to put Maple Woods behind him, and get out of town no sooner than he had returned, it seemed like wishful thinking that he might ever be back again.

She began to measure out the sugar thoughtfully, reminding herself that she might not be in town much longer, either. Some things just weren't meant to be.

Scott locked the door to the apartment above the diner where Lucy was letting him stay and jogged down the stairs to Main Street. He eyed the bakery across the street and wavered slightly, wondering if he should give in to the temptation of what was tucked inside, his mind on anything but the pie.

Quickly, he looked away, assessing his options. He'd slept late, and by the time he'd dragged himself out of the comfortable solitude of his room, it was already nearing lunchtime. He was prolonging the inevitable trek to his father's office, but eventually he would have to head over—there was no getting around it.

Once he thought he would continue the legacy of Collins Construction, follow in the footsteps of his father and grandfather. Back then his plan was simple: he would marry Emily Porter, settle down in Maple Woods and earn an honest living at his family's company. But that was before he knew what his family had done to Emily's. Before he knew the part he had played in her father's death when he was just a kid, playing on the machinery, hanging out on his dad's job site, too oblivious to know the truth. Before he knew there was nothing honest about that company. Or his father. Or himself.

"Scott!" Lucy's familiar voice jarred him. He hated to think what her opinion must be of him now—she probably assumed he had gotten too successful for a small town like this, that he was better than it somehow, that he couldn't be bothered to make time for people who had meant so much to him in the past, including her. She couldn't be more wrong.

It was easier this way, he told himself, better that she wasn't in on the family secret. It was easier for everyone he cared about to be left out of his mess. Let them think he went off to college and never looked back, that he didn't think of Maple Woods every damn day of his life, that he didn't wonder how different things might have been. Let them think he was happy in Seattle, that city life fit him in a way Maple Woods never could. Let them all think what they wanted, so long as they didn't know the real reason he had left.

A man was dead because of him, and the surviving family had suffered as a result.

He forced a smile and crossed the street to stand next to his sister. "I was thinking about grabbing something to eat at the diner," he said as he approached the sidewalk.

"You're not sick of my cooking after dinner last night?"

Scott smiled at the recollection of sitting around Lucy's old farm table with her husband and son, talking and laughing long into the night like any other family would. A few times he'd caught himself thinking that maybe he could have a life like this, but that must have been the wine talking. There was no room for him in this place.

"I haven't had a meal like that in years." He grinned.

"Well, you can have another tonight, then. I'm going over to Mom and Dad's for dinner after work."

Scott's gut twisted as he held her eyes, carefully selecting his excuse. Lucy stood before him unwavering, her mouth a thin line. She knew what she was doing. And he didn't like it one bit.

"Lucy, don't do this to me." He sighed, running a hand through his hair in agitation. He broke her gaze and glanced down the street, desperate for an escape.

Her eyes were sharp when he turned his attention back to her. "Dad's dying, Scott," she said firmly, her gaze narrowing in disappointment. "The treatments aren't working. The cancer has spread."

"You know we don't get along," Scott insisted, but Lucy was shaking her head, clearly not buying it.

"Scott, I've put up with this nonsense for long enough," she said, her voice steely. "Whatever happened between you and our parents is old news. You were a teenager then, now you're a thirty-year-old man. Start acting like one," she snapped.

Scott took a step back, his eyes flashing with indignation. He forced himself to remember that Lucy didn't know the part his father had played in the events of the past. He'd kept in touch with her over the years, but he made sure to keep their conversations light, and mostly about her, George and Bobby. "You know I came back for you. You asked for my help in the rebuilding of the library, and I'm here. I'll see it through, but please don't ask anything more."

Lucy's eyes softened. "I know, and I'm so grateful, Scott. Honestly, I am." She lowered her eyes to the ground, her shoulders slumping. "I've lived with so much guilt knowing that Bobby accidentally caused that fire." She shook her head. "I just don't know what we would have done if Max Hamilton wasn't funding the project in exchange for some land George inherited. You can't imagine how that felt...the *relief.*"

No, Scott thought grimly. He couldn't say he did know how that would feel. There was no stranger to swoop into town and clear up his mess, the way Max had apparently helped so much since moving to Maple Woods after the holidays. Scott couldn't rebuild the past. He couldn't raise the dead. There was no righting his wrongs.

"It means everything to me that you're here to take over the job, Scott. Don't lose sight of that," she explained.

Scott eyed her warily. "I sense a 'but' coming on."

Lucy gave a sad smile. "Don't let this chance pass you by. It's been a long time. Let things go. Don't do something you'll regret forever." She held his gaze, and he almost felt his stance weaken, his resolve waver. Almost.

Scott shook his head adamantly, feeling the flush of heat spread up his neck. "I don't regret staying away, Lucy." And he didn't. His father might not have trouble looking people in the eye, knowing the part he played in one of the town's greatest tragedies, but Scott would rather give up everything he loved than build his life around a lie.

"Well, if you can't do it for yourself, then do it for

me!" she said, her eyes suddenly filling with tears as fury blazed bright.

Scott cursed inwardly, feeling the strain of her emotion, the weight of his burden. After a long pause, he said tightly, "No promises."

Lucy relaxed her stance. She nodded slowly, saying nothing more as she reached out to take his arm. It took everything in him not to break down then and there, to tell her everything. To shed the weight he had carried for so long. To divulge every last detail of what his parents told him that awful night—what their family had done to the Porters. *Those poor Porters.*

"Come into the bakery," she said to him. "We've got a special event as part of the opening week and I don't want you to miss it."

Scott hesitated. "You're not working at the diner this morning?"

"Not if I can help it." Lucy bent down to clip a sprig of blue hydrangea from a whiskey barrel planter. "I barely spent an hour at Sweetie Pie without being interrupted yesterday, they were so lost without me at the diner. I'm hoping things go a little smoother today."

Without another word, she pushed through the front door, frowning until Scott forced himself to follow. His pulse skipped when he saw Emily standing behind the counter, looking just as pretty as the day before. She met his gaze with a small smile and something deep within his gut stirred. He looked away, around the crowded room, noticing that nearly every table was filled. There was a cheerful buzz to the room, a soft tinkling of music in the background, and the sweet aroma of pie and coffee to make everyone, including him, feel at home.

Home. He hadn't thought of that word in a very long time. It was a vague idea of something he wasn't sure he had anymore. He hadn't dared to think of Maple Woods as home since he'd left, and his condo in Seattle was just a place to live.

"Emily!" Lucy called to Scott's horror. His breath locked in his tightened chest. "Mind getting Scott settled? I've got to check on that order of strawberries. We should have had them an hour ago."

Emily's face blanched and she darted her gaze from Lucy to Scott and back again. "Sure," she murmured as she finished plating a slice of pie for an impatient customer.

Scott turned to his sister. "I came in here to visit with you, Lucy," he said quietly.

"Emily will take good care of you. If you let her." Lucy winked.

"What's that supposed to mean?" he shot back.

"I'm just saying that Emily makes a damn good pie," she said airily. "Last I checked, that was the purest way to a man's heart."

Scott chuckled in spite of himself. "Lucy! Please!"

"What? I seem to remember you being awfully smitten with her at one point. I always thought you were going to marry her, in fact." She lifted an eyebrow and turned away from him with a coy shrug, shutting down the conversation.

Scott shook his head and reluctantly walked over to the display case, sparing an awkward smile for Emily. Guilt and shame haunted him, and he tried desperately to shrug off the unwanted feelings.

"Hi." Emily's soft voice dragged him from his darkening thoughts and he quickly recovered, perking up as he let his gaze roam over her pretty face. His stomach tightened as his attention lingered on the smoky gray eyes and that plump, upturned mouth stained a shade of red that excited him more than it should.

"Hey." He stared into his mug as she filled it to the rim. Just the way he liked it. His breath hitched as he caught sight of her feminine curves beneath the apron she wore, and he tried to recall what it had felt like to hold her waist and feel her body against his. The memory was so close, but just out of reach.

She held his gaze, not betraying any outward interest, and Scott felt a flicker of disappointment. She was being hospitable. Playing her role. Doing her job. He wanted to pull her into a back room, somewhere they could talk, and explain everything. He wanted to atone for the pain he had caused, to make it up to her—somehow. He searched her face, imagining her sweet expression crumbling before his eyes as he delivered the crushing news, and his gut twisted. He couldn't do it, he just couldn't, but to never tell her…

"So, I don't see you for twelve years and now it's twice in two days," she said, shaking her head on a sigh. "The pie must be even better than I thought."

Scott grimaced at the edge of hurt in her tone and took a quick sip of the steaming coffee. "Lucy invited me in," he began. "I don't want to upset you. I can leave if you want."

Fire sparked her eyes. "Leave?" She chuckled, a soft icy sound that pulled at his chest. She really did hate him, and who could blame her? "Leaving seems to be something you've had practice with," she said evenly.

Scott drew a ragged breath and ran a hand over his face, every inch of his heart aching to set her straight, to tell her the truth. It wasn't supposed to be this way.

"Believe it or not I had my reasons." He cleared his throat and finished the rest of his coffee. His body temperature was starting to rise. He needed to get out of here. Even his father's office would be better than this place. Anything was better than seeing that hurt expression in Emily's eyes.

Emily leaned a hip against the counter and folded her arms. "I'm all ears."

The knot in his gut tightened. Not now. Not like this. Not ever. Emily could never know what he had done, the part he had played in her misfortune. The losses she had suffered at his hand. "It was a long time ago, Em," he finally said.

After a beat, she gave him a withering smile and slapped a hand over his empty mug, pulling it toward her. "You're right," she said, before turning her back on him. "And I stopped holding my breath before you'd even crossed the state line."

He scowled. "You don't mean that."

"Is it really so hard to believe?" She snatched a rag from under the counter and began scrubbing furiously at the polished wood counter. "We were kids, Scott. It was a fling, it was fun, and then it was over."

"Emily." She couldn't mean those harsh words. She couldn't. They'd been in love. "It wasn't a fling."

She stopped scrubbing, but her hand remained clenched on the rag. "Maybe it wasn't. But it was just as meaningless in the end."

She turned on her heel and walked away before he could open his mouth to reply. From the entrance to the kitchen, Scott saw Lucy smiling at him, her eyes full of hope. He wrapped a hand around his neck and rubbed at the tense and aching muscles.

If Lucy thought she was playing matchmaker here, she was doing a very bad job of it.

The nerve of that man!

Emily's blood pounded in her ears as she assisted the next customer on autopilot. From the corner of her eye she could see Scott, sitting at the counter, fingers tented before him, his mouth a thin, grim line.

What was he still doing here? Why wouldn't he just leave?

She lifted her chin and turned away from him once more, denying the temptation to steal another glance. So he knew he had hurt her, knew how badly he had broken her heart. And now—now!—he wanted to spare her? As if he assumed she was still holding on, still licking her wounds from a dozen years ago.

She gritted her teeth. He knew her better than she wished he did in that moment.

She turned her head slightly, waiting to take another quick peek, her pulse quickening as she did so. Yep, still there all right. Well, no bother. He was here for Lucy, after all. And the freaking pie. Honestly!

He looked up, catching her stare. Flustered, Emily spilled the coffee she had been pouring all over the counter. She hissed out a curse and grabbed a rag, hiding her burning face behind the curtain of hair spilling from her ponytail as she wiped up her mess, trying to ignore the tremble in her hand.

Damn you, Scott Collins! After everything he had done to her—the way he had treated her—she was still irresistibly, hopelessly, foolishly attracted to this man.

A commotion was starting near the door and Emily looked up to see Jack Logan and Cole Davis hollering to Scott, both men grinning ear to ear as they strode past the counter and greeted the town's prodigal son with slaps on the back and high fives. Emily bit back a scowl. The kid who put Maple Woods on the map with that tie breaking touchdown senior year had graced them with his presence. A photograph of Scott's victorious win still hung in the principal's office.

She listened passively as the men caught up, making promises to meet up for beers one night, to talk about the good ol' times. Her heart fell, wondering why the same hadn't been offered to her. Hadn't she been just as much of a mark on that time in his life as his teammates? Hadn't she been more?

"Emily, we have a problem," Lucy announced, coming out of the kitchen flushed and breathless.

Emily studied her in alarm. "What is it?" she asked, realizing that Scott had stopped talking with Jack and Cole long enough to eavesdrop.

"It's the mayor. He has a last-minute meeting. He isn't going to make it." She gestured around the packed room of customers, all waiting for a chance to partake in the pie toss. "I hate to let them down. Our first week in business!"

Emily opened her mouth to put her boss at ease when Scott cut in. "What's the problem, Lucy?" he asked.

Emily trained her eye on Lucy, refusing to feed into his concern. So he felt like being nice now. Felt like playing hero. Where was this chivalry twelve years ago? Where was his sense of responsibility then?

"It's the pie toss," Lucy explained. "We seem to be missing our target."

"Let Scott do it!" Jack suggested, and Cole laughed heartily, slapping Scott soundly on the back.

The men grabbed his shoulders, cajoled him until his face was red and his smile was broad enough to reveal that elusive dimple she had almost managed to forget. He held up his hands in mock defeat. "Okay, okay," he said, grinning. "But only as a favor for my sister."

A cheer went up in the room at this and Lucy beamed, leading the group through the front door to where a chair had been set up on the sidewalk for all of Maple Woods to see. If this didn't pique interest and generate business, Emily wasn't sure what would. Already a few curious customers from Lucy's Place had emerged from the open door, lifting their chins to take in the show across the street.

"Don't go too easy on the whipped cream," Jack advised her, and she slid him a smile. Oh, she didn't intend to. "Hey," he said, tipping his head. "Didn't you and Scott used to date?"

Emily felt her cheeks warm, but before she had a chance to shut down the question, Jack turned to Scott, who was settling himself into the folding chair. "It's a real reunion over here, today. You and Emily used to date, didn't you?"

Emily filled another pie plate, holding her breath. Seconds seemed to pass as she waited for Scott's answer, her heart racing with expectation.

"Yeah, we used to hang out," he finally said.

Her hands went still. They used to *hang out?* Three years of her life, all those days spent laughing and talking, curling into each other's arms, dreaming of a future. They were just hanging out!

Tears prickled the backs of her eyes, whether from fury or sadness, she wasn't even sure anymore. She thought it had hurt when he disappeared without a trace twelve years ago, but hearing him dismiss their relationship all over again only broke her heart for the second time.

She set the pie plate down and turned to him, resting her hands on her hips. Watching him sit there with that expectant grin on his face that used to be reserved just for her, practically basking in the attention of half the town who had gathered to see Scott Collins—back at long last!—she felt her heart begin to rip all over again.

"Who's up first?" Lucy called out, and a shuffling and nervous laughter fell over the crowd.

"Why don't I kick this off?" Emily heard herself say.

Scott swiveled to her. Dread clouded his eyes, but there was no denying the amused twitch in that cocky grin.

Setting her jaw, Emily swiftly picked up a pie plate and walked to the line Lucy had drawn out in white chalk. Without waiting for a signal, she hurled the plate in Scott's direction. Whipped cream splattered at his feet.

A rumble went up in the crowd, but Emily barely noticed it. Her chest heaved with each breath as she stared at him, remembering the way his mouth used to curve when he saw her across the room, the way his brow would lift ever so slightly, the way he would quietly come up to her and place one hand on her hip. Lifting her chin, Emily marched back into the bakery, ignoring the way the crowd hushed and then slowly started to whisper with speculation. She walked around the counter, grabbed Scott's beloved cherry pie from its stand, and beelined back to the door. An audible gasp released from the crowd as she stepped onto the sidewalk, but they were of no concern to her at the moment. There was only one person on her mind, and he had it coming. This was well overdue.

"Emily—" Scott's old buddy Jack started, but she nailed him with a hard look and he clamped his mouth.

She positioned herself before she lost her nerve, but the adrenaline pumping in her veins showed no signs of slowing. She locked eyes with her target, noticing the way his brow had furrowed to a point. He let out a nervous chuckle. *This is for stealing my heart, Scott.* She pulled her arm back, fixing her eye on that lopsided grin that quickly vanished as she released the aluminum pan, sending it flying in his direction. *And that's for breaking it.*

She knew even before it hit him square in the face that her aim was perfect. And he knew it, too—she saw his expression dissolve into one of frozen shock just before the pie slammed into him, dead center, knocking him slightly to the left. Bright red filling oozed from the sides of the flimsy pan as it slowly slid down his nose. Scott swiped at the cherries and bits of crust that clung to his face, his eyes wide and confused, and for a moment, Emily almost felt sorry for what she had done. But then she remembered. He was no friend of hers. And she had nothing to apologize for. That was his department.

The crowd was laughing now, but Emily wasn't amused. Blindly muttering something to Lucy about going back inside to man the counter, she wove through the throng of onlookers, ducked into the empty storefront, and pushed past the swinging door to the kitchen. And only then, only when she was sure no one would ever see or ever know, did she allow herself to cry over Scott Collins.

Chapter Three

Scott pulled his car to a stop and shut off the ignition, sighing as he leaned back against the smooth leather headrest. The evening sunlight reflected off the windows of his parents' house, making it impossible to see inside. He felt an odd sensation of disbelief that he had once lived here at all, much less that he had spent the first eighteen years of his life knowing every inch of the house by heart, thinking of it as home. Still one of the prettiest houses in all of Maple Woods, time was obviously posing a challenge for its upkeep: white paint peeled from various corners of the siding; grass was sprouting up through a few cracks in the brick path leading up to the center door; the yard needed weeding and the bushes needed to be pruned.

Lucy's car was parked at the top of the driveway, and Scott couldn't fight the twinge of resentment he felt toward her. She had won—dragged him here against his will. She didn't understand the circumstances that had kept him away, but why the heck couldn't she just respect his wishes? Wasn't he doing enough for her already?

Scott gritted his teeth. *It's now or never.* He pulled on the latch and thrust the car door open, closing it behind him with quiet force. Shoving his hands into his pockets, he strode up the cracking path to the faded green door, wondering if he should knock or just try the handle. Hesitating, he knocked twice, peering through the slender window that framed the door for any sign of activity inside. Seconds later, an older woman with gray hair and a plump middle entered the front hall. When she saw him through the glass, she stopped walking and her hand flew to her heart.

His mother.

Instinctively, he pulled back from the window. He ran his fingers coarsely through his hair. The last time he had seen her she was an attractive woman in her late forties. Now she was sixty. Rationally he knew it had been a long time. He just hadn't realized the toll the years had taken on her.

The door flung open and his mother's bright blue eyes locked with his. Blinking back tears, she leaned forward and grabbed him, squeezing him tight to a body that still felt familiar.

As soon as he could, he pulled back, standing uncomfortably in the door frame, allowing her gaze to roam over him with nostalgic appraisal, as though she had just stumbled upon a once-cherished childhood toy in the attic. He hated this. He *hated* this. He had thought he had cut off his feelings a long time ago—that he would be strong enough to deal with this reunion if it ever came—but the ache in his chest proved otherwise.

"It's so good to see you," his mother said breathlessly, and Scott managed a weak smile.

"The house looks nice," he offered, stepping into the hall. He glanced around. Everything was exactly the same. Every painting hung on its same hook, every chair sat planted in the same position. Yet somehow, it was all different.

"Ah well, I've been meaning to get someone out here to take care of the yard now that..." she trailed off and inhaled sharply, closing the door behind him and then smoothing her hands over her skirt.

Scott balled his hands at his sides. "Is Lucy in the kitchen?" he asked, following the smell that was wafting from the back of the house.

Lucy was standing at the big island in the middle of the room, tossing a salad. Her eyes were unnaturally bright when she smiled. When she said hello, her voice was a notch higher than usual. It was then that he realized she was nervous. Well, she was the one insisting on this awkward arrangement. He wasn't sure why she thought it would be easy. For any of them.

"I see you're all cleaned up," she observed.

Scott shrugged. He had hoped to avoid thinking of Emily for just one night, but that was impossible. Being here in this house only stirred his emotions to the surface. "Keep tossing pies at me and I'll never get into the office to get the library project under way," he warned.

"Don't worry," Lucy replied. "That's it for the promotional stunts. But between you and me, I think you were a bigger hit than the mayor would have been."

"Glad I could help." He glanced around the room. "Where are George and Bobby?"

"George's at the diner. Bobby's studying for a test tomorrow."

Scott nodded. Topic closed, the room fell silent again. He released a heavy sigh. "Where's..."

"Dad?" Lucy lifted an eyebrow. Tight-lipped, she returned her attention to the salad. "He's upstairs."

His mother appeared in the arched doorway that led to the dining room. "He's so pleased to know you're here," she added.

That makes one of us.

Scott rolled his shoulders, pushing back the resentment. He was angry at his parents—angry to the bone—but damn it if a part of him didn't ache when he thought of them. It was easier, with time and distance, to just focus on the bad—on the event that had severed his ties with them for good. But all it took was one hint of his mother's smile, the lull of her voice, to make him wish with all his might that things could have been different, that he could have just loved his parents and let them love him. That he didn't have to look at them and be reminded of everything that had been lost instead.

He set his jaw and turned to the window, looking out over the backyard that stretched to the wood. Tulips had sprung up around the edges of the house providing a cheerful contrast to the situation within.

"Your father won't be able to come down for dinner," his mother was saying as she pulled three place mats from the basket on the baker's rack. "We'll take some soup up to him after he rests."

They wandered silently into the dining room, his mother taking her usual place at the head of the table closest to the kitchen, he and Lucy sliding into their childhood seats on autopilot. Scott unfolded the thick cloth napkin and placed it in his lap. "Looks delicious, Lucy," he said as she handed him a plate with a large steaming square of lasagna.

"Lucy's been keeping us well fed," his mother said through a tight smile. "More food than one person can eat, really," she continued, her voice growing sad. "Have you been over to the office yet?" his mother continued.

It both amazed and saddened Scott that his relationship with his mother had come to this: polite, stilted conversation. As though there was never a bond between them—not a shared love, not a shared life, not a shared secret.

He took a bite of the lasagna. "Not yet." He forced his tone not to turn bitter when he said, "Given Dad's commitment to the company, I think it's safe to assume everything is in place for the library project and I can just take over where he left off." A heavy silence fell over the room.

Lucy bit on her lip and then asked tentatively, "Why don't you go upstairs and see him after we're finished with dinner?"

His stomach twisted, but he nodded. Wordlessly, he finished his meal, slowly pushed back his chair and followed his mother up the stairs, his pulse taking speed with each step. He kept his gaze low, noticing how the floorboards creaked under the weight of each step. Lucy stayed downstairs, under the guise of cleaning up the kitchen, but he knew better. She was down there wringing her hands, saying a hundred desperate prayers that progress would be made, and that all would be forgotten.

Oh, Lucy.

"He might be sleeping," his mother whispered as they approached the master bedroom. She stopped, her hand clutching the brass knob. "Let me just go in and tell him you're here."

Scott stepped back and his mother slipped through the door, leaving it open an inch. Through the crack he could hear her soothing voice telling his father that "Scottie" was home and wanted to see him. If his father said anything in return, it wasn't audible from this distance.

His mother tipped her head around the door frame and nodded. With one last sharp breath, Scott entered the room, his blood stilling at what he saw. His father, once a strapping, robust man with a handsome face and personality that could intimidate even the strongest of men on a construction crew, had withered into a frail wisp of his former self. His skin, once bronzed from days spent on job sites, was now an alarming shade of grayish-white. Propped up on two pillows, his eyes were hollow and dark.

Scott crossed the room, his body numb.

"Dad."

"I knew you would come home." His father's voice strained with effort, but it was still deep, still authoritative. "I knew someday you would put this business with the Porters behind you and finally come home."

Scott's pulse hammered. "I haven't put this business with the Porters behind me and I never will," he said evenly.

"Scott!" his mother cried out, but he couldn't stop now if he wanted to. Even now, after all this time, the man still refused to acknowledge what he had done. The part he had played.

"A man died," Scott insisted, silently pleading with his father to set things right once and for all. "A man with two daughters and a wife. And I was the one who took him from them," Scott said quietly, feeling the anger uncoil in his stomach as the words spilled out. "You knew I was responsible for the accident that day and you kept that information from everyone. From the police. From Lucy. Even from me."

"You were nine years old, Scott. We were just trying to protect you—"

"No." Scott shook his head forcefully, trying to drive out the words, the excuses. "I should go, Dad." *Before I say anything I'll regret.* "You need your rest."

Scott paused with his hand on the door, and then slipped into the hall. His mother grabbed him by the elbow.

"Thank you for seeing him, Scott. It means so much to us."

Scott's eyes flashed on his mother. "Why can't he just admit it, Mom? Why can't you? You denied the Porter family insurance money that was owed them."

She visibly paled and looked away. "It was an *accident,* Scott."

"Maybe so, but it didn't have to happen. I had no business being on the machinery that day. A nine-year-old kid shouldn't be on a job site." He shook his head. "If I had never overhead you talking about it all those years later, would you ever have told me that I was the one responsible for the accident?"

His mother hesitated. "Probably not. You were already upset by the commotion that day. And what were we supposed to tell you? You were nine, Scott. We didn't want you or your sister to have to live with this. Lucy still doesn't know," she added.

"I'm aware of that," Scott said, "and I don't intend to burden her with this.

"Then you can understand how we felt. We were trying to protect you."

"By blaming the victim?" Scott cried.

"We never could have recovered from a lawsuit. Richard Porter was gone. There was nothing we could do to bring him back."

"Then you admit it. You chose to protect yourself financially."

"We chose to protect the company financially," his mother corrected him. "Nearly a third of the men in this town were employed by Collins Construction. They had wives and children—families of their own, depending on that paycheck. Would it have been better to make them all suffer?"

"So it was fair for Emily's family to suffer? They had nothing. Nothing!"

It was a no-win situation, he knew that now. A man was dead, his family impoverished and the only way they would have been reimbursed was for others to suffer at their expense. The only way everyone could have been spared was if Scott had never been on that machine that day. If his father hadn't let him tag along to work.

"We covered the funeral expenses," his mother offered, and Scott clenched a fist, willing himself not to lose his temper.

"It doesn't change the fact that we are all living this lie! The police took Dad's statement for the events of that day. Collins Construction had just finished building that addition on the Maple Woods police station—at cost. He knew they wouldn't pursue a criminal investigation when everyone was pointing the finger at Mr. Porter's negligence, and so it all just went away. And Emily and her family were not only denied the money they were rightfully owed for their father's wrongful death, but worse—" his throat locked up when he thought of it "—is that you allowed them to think their father's carelessness led to his death."

"It wasn't easy for us, either. We thought you would never have to know your part in this. And then all those years later you had to go and start dating Emily Porter. Of all people! Believe me when I say we *never* intended you to know the truth, especially when we saw how much you cared for her."

Scott lowered his voice. "You *knew* how much she meant to me, and you never even welcomed her into our home."

"You didn't honestly think we were going to be able to invite that girl into our lives, feeling the reminder every day of what we did."

Scott narrowed his eyes. "And here I thought you walked away with a clear conscience."

His mother stared at him levelly. "My conscience will never be free."

"Well, that makes two of us," Scott retorted. He ran a hand through his hair. "I have to go," he said, taking a step back, and then another. This was a useless, maddening effort.

"What are you doing?" Lucy cried in alarm, her face pale, her expression stricken as he bolted down the stairs.

"I shouldn't have come here!" he said, bursting past her toward the front door. "Now do you see?"

"What is *wrong* with you?" Lucy hissed. "Our father is dying. Do you hear me? *Dying.* Why can't you get over yourself for once and be the bigger person?"

Scott whipped around and met his sister's desperate gaze. "Lucy, when it comes to our parents, I do not want to hear another word about my relationship with them. Not. One. Word."

"You're a jerk," Lucy snapped.

Scott hesitated. "I'm worse than that."

"What's that supposed to mean?"

Scott shook his head. "You have no idea."

Lucy's voice softened. "Try me."

"Forget it," he said, striding for the door. He placed his hand on the knob and twisted it, hesitating. Turning to face Lucy again, his gut tightened at the sight of her anguished face. "I'm sorry you got dragged into all of this, Lucy," he said, closing the door behind him.

The spring air was cool and fresh on his lungs, and crickets chirped in the distance. He ran his hands down his face, staring at his ludicrous rental car, so sleek and bold and out of place. The image of his father lying in that bed was too clear to banish, but the words were what haunted him the most. What had he been expecting? He grimaced to think a part of him had wanted the same thing as Lucy. Closure. Peace. Some glimmer of relief to this endless, lifelong misery that hung over their family like a plague. And now he knew, perhaps he always had though, and that's why he had stayed away. It just was what it was.

"I just don't know what came over me," Emily repeated, closing her eyes to the memory of her outburst that afternoon.

"Well, I do!" Julia declared. "The man had it coming, Emily."

"But, Julia, I work there. That's my boss's brother!"

Julia waved her hand through the air. "Please. Lucy knows you and Scott have a history. Besides, she was the one who commissioned him for the contest."

Emily considered her sister's reasoning. "Maybe you're right," she said quietly.

"Maybe? Emily, Scott Collins is a *jerk*," Julia said firmly. "I'm so sick of hearing everyone in town go on and on about his return. If it were up to me, he'd never have come back. Seriously, I mean who does he think he is, huh? He might have been Mr. Popularity back in high school, but he's thirty years old now and he needs to get over himself. But one day he'll see that he can't just tromp around on his high horse, zipping through town in his fancy car, flashing that smile and expecting every woman in the street to just *swoon*. Oh, what I wouldn't like to do to him…just kick that butt right to the curb, right out of Maple Woods, back to wherever the heck it is he's been hiding all this time…"

Emily heaved a sigh and glanced at her sister, whose eyes had narrowed to green slits, her pink lips pinched in fury as she detailed the revenge she'd like to take on Scott Collins, and burst out laughing. It was the first good laugh Emily had enjoyed all day, and she needed it more than she'd realized. "Are you finished?" she asked, when she'd settled down.

"It's not funny!" Julia exclaimed, shaking her head in disgust. She leaned over and took a long sip of wine from her glass and then set it back down on the coffee table with a scowl. She reached for her knitting needles and motioned to Emily to flick on the television. The sisters had just finished eating dinner and were getting ready to catch up on the soap opera that they recorded each afternoon and watched together each night. It was a cozy ritual, and one that Emily cherished, even if she sometimes did worry that she and Julia were destined to become two spinsters, living in a four-room apartment above the town diner for the rest of their lives.

Emily's stomach tightened. There was still a chance that she would get into that school in Boston. Today's mail had brought no news with it, but eventually an answer would arrive. The anticipation of opening the mailbox each day was starting to become almost too much. For so long she had dreamed of the opportunity to leave Maple Woods, to go out into the world and begin her own life, to put everything she hated about this town behind her. She longed to start fresh. She was a person in her own right, and the longer she still lived with the weight of her family's past, the more she resented the town that had defined her by it.

She had applied to the school with big dreams and a flutter of hope that caused her heart to soar. Now that the thought of leaving Maple Woods and everyone in it was becoming a possibility, she began to wonder if she could really go through with it.

She glanced at Julia, then swept her gaze over the

small room that housed a hand-me-down couch and coffee table, and an old television propped on some milk crates. *Be real.* If this was all Maple Woods could offer her, then she had no other choice. If she got accepted to the school in Boston, she was going.

"I guess Scott had it coming." Emily sighed as she settled back against a couch cushion and tucked her feet under her. It felt so good to sit down. Between the anxiety of waiting for the mail each day, the stress of seeing Scott and the long hours at the bakery, she felt as if she could shut her eyes and fall asleep right then and there. And it was only eight o'clock!

"Oh, he had it coming," Julia insisted, wide-eyed, and Emily bit back a smile at the indignation in her voice. She was a girl of principles, and Emily loved her for it. It was something she was going to miss if she left—she really needed to stop thinking that way.

"Still, I guess we can't exactly call him a jerk for not being interested in me," Emily summarized.

"Oh, yes we can!" Julia slammed a bamboo knitting needle down on the coffee table and reached for her wineglass again. "You dated for three years and he up and disappears. Just...vanishes. Then he saunters back into town without so much as an explanation?" She shook her head. "I'm sorry, Emily, but you're too forgiving. I saw how crushed you were when he left, even though you tried to hide it from me."

Emily eyed her sister coolly, taking a sip of wine from her own glass. Julia didn't remember their father's funeral as well as she did—she was only six at the time, while Emily was already eight. Emily had cried herself to sleep for at least a year after that day, and she knew that no other heartache could ever be as painful as losing her dad. When Scott had left, it didn't seem right to cry for him—he had chosen to leave her after all, he wasn't taken from her. He wasn't worth her tears, she'd told herself firmly, but then today, after all this time, she finally released the pain she'd been holding inside.

"You're right," she suddenly said, flashing Julia a conspiratorial grin. Her sister's eyes gleamed in return. "He is a jerk."

"Thatta girl." Julia winked and, satisfied, snuggled back on the couch with her sister as the opening credits to the soap opera started. They watched in silence, fast-forwarding through the commercials, occasionally gasping at some dramatic turn in events. They had grown up with these characters—had watched them every day after school together while they did housework and got dinner ready. Some people thought growing up in Maple Woods was boring. Small-town life. No excitement or fun. The Porter girls had enough uncertainty in their young lives to make up for the shortcomings the town experienced in general. This television show, while silly, was one constant they had over time.

"My prediction for tomorrow?" Julia reached for the remote and turned off the television. "Brad's not the father."

Emily's mouth curled into a smile. "Ooooh. I like that!" The sisters giggled.

They began gathering up their dinner plates and glasses, both groaning as they sauntered into the kitchen and noticed the pile of dishes from what had seemed like such a basic pasta recipe, and begrudgingly started rinsing the pots when the sound of heavy footsteps on the other side of the door caused them each to freeze midtask.

Emily's heart began to pound, even though she rationally knew she was being ridiculous. This was Maple Woods. There was no crime here. The last instance of a burglary had been at the penny candy shop on Oak and Birch, when little Molly Roberts plucked a lollipop from the counter and ran off to the park.

Standing at the sink, Emily glanced sidelong at her sister and met her fearful gaze. "Did Lucy mention that someone was staying in the spare room down the hall?" Julia whispered.

Emily shook her head and peered into the soapy water and tried to remember if Lucy had ever hinted at such a thing. Surely she would have mentioned something like this, even if it was just to ask Emily to give a friendly wave to the newcomer. Maple Woods was small, and in the six months since Julia and Emily had moved into the apartment above the diner that Lucy and George had lived in for the first five years of their marriage, no one else had come through the second floor of the building. There was only one other apartment and it was just a room really that Lucy kept on hand for guests.

Guests. The air tightened in Emily's lungs. Without another glance at her sister, Emily wiped her hands dry on a dishtowel and tossed it on the counter. *Of course.*

Straightening her spine, she lifted her chin, marched the eight feet to the front door of the apartment and flung it open.

Scott's face blanched and his wide blue eyes shifted from her to the door at the end of the hall and back again. "Emily. What are you doing here?"

"I live here," she said calmly, even though her pulse was doing jumping jacks.

He combed a hand through his hair and chuckled. "George and Lucy's old apartment... I'm staying in the spare room at the end of the hall."

"I figured as much. It was either that or a break-in."

His frown deepened. "Oh. Sorry about that. I... Well, I should let you get back to your evening. You're probably busy."

Emily opened her mouth to respond but Julia's voice purred smoothly from behind her. "Oh, but quite the contrary."

Emily whipped around and flashed a warning look at her sister, who pretended not to catch it.

"It isn't often we're graced with the talk of the town." Julia smiled sweetly, and Emily closed her eyes, bracing herself. "Please, Scott. Come in. We have a lot of catching up to do and I was just about to put the water on for tea."

Scott cupped his tea and saucer in his lap and glanced up at Julia. She'd grown up from a freckle-faced, scrawny little teenager into a striking beauty with creamy skin and distinct coloring. Deep auburn hair and green cat eyes stared back at him.

"So, Scott," she said, setting down her mismatched cup to pick up her knitting. "I heard Emily really let you have it today."

She arched an eyebrow as her lips curled mischievously, and it was then that he realized she was talking about the pie toss. He chuckled, feeling some of the nervous energy roll off him. "Ah well, it was all in good fun. It washed off."

Julia's eyes were sharp. "Not quite the same as a dagger to the heart, I suppose."

"Julia!" Emily snapped, but Julia just pinched her lips and casually returned to her knitting.

"You'll have to forgive my sister," Emily said, reddening.

Scott shrugged. "I probably deserved that one."

"My goodness!" Julia snorted. "Is that actual remorse I detect?"

"Julia!" Emily said sharply. "Don't you have to finish knitting those cashmere socks for the window display at the shop?"

Julia let out a sigh. "I know when to take a hint." She stood, gathering her yarn in her hands. "Besides, you two have unfinished business to discuss."

She held Scott's gaze as she retreated from the room, and he made a mental note to steer clear of her until she'd calmed down.

He waited until he heard the door click shut, but as he looked down the hall to make sure, he noticed the brass handle silently turn, and the door to Julia's room remained open exactly an inch after that.

"Sorry about that," Emily said as he settled back against his chair. She rubbed her forehead, something he remembered she did when she was feeling stressed.

"She's protective of you," he said affably. "I think it's sweet."

Emily dropped her hand, spearing him with a sharp look. "I can fight my own battles."

She sat less than three feet from him, but the distance felt much greater as she stared at him flatly, her eyes sad and tired, her face pale. She looked weary and exhausted and Scott had never felt like a bigger jerk in all his life. He had intruded on her home, interrupted her evening and now he was sitting in the heated silence of her living room like an unwanted piece of furniture.

He glanced around the small room, sweeping his view into the adjoining kitchen. A small hallway led to two rooms that scarcely qualified as bedrooms and a shared bathroom. He hadn't been in this place in years—not since Lucy and George moved in when they were first married at barely the age of twenty. It seemed bigger then. Special and grown-up.

"So how long have you lived here?" he asked, hoping to lighten the mood.

Emily heaved a sigh. "Julia and I moved in about six months ago when our mother sold the house and moved down to Florida to be with our aunt. It's small, but it's convenient."

He stole another glance at the living room. It was cramped but cozy, but not cozy enough to make him wish this on her. If she'd been able to go to college, instead of sticking around to support her mother, she would have had more options. Instead… He set his cup on the coffee table.

"I should probably get going," he said, pulling himself to his feet. "Please thank your sister for the tea."

"Are you kidding me?" Emily's tone shattered the silent chill of the room. "That's all you have to say?"

No, it wasn't all he had to say. He had a lot more to say. A hell of a lot more. Things he'd been aching to say for years. Things he'd kept bottled up. Things he'd tried to bury.

Scott drew a ragged breath. "It's late," he settled on. He would make things right with Emily, but what that entailed he wasn't yet sure. All he knew was that tonight the best thing he could do was to walk out the door and leave her alone. "I should go."

"This seems to be the way you operate." She crossed her arms over her chest. Against the well-worn floorboards, her bare foot tapped expectantly. Unable to resist, Scott let his gaze trace the curve of her calf to her toes. He swallowed hard and forced himself to look back to her face as heat rushed to his groin.

"What's that supposed to mean?"

Emily's shadowed gaze remained cool and steady until she abruptly shifted her eyes to the clock on top of a nearby bookshelf. She shook her head and, standing, muttered, "Forget it."

"No, I can't forget it," Scott said. "I've never forgotten it. Any of it. Emily, I can explain—" He stopped himself. He could explain, of course he could, but explaining why he had so abruptly broken up with her would entail telling her about the horrible, tragic, irreversible thing he had done.

She chewed at her bottom lip, sizing him up, deciding perhaps if she wanted to hear what he had to say, or if she'd rather let it go.

"Forget it," she said again, this time through a sigh of disgust that punched him straight in the gut. "Actions speak louder than words. You didn't even say goodbye, Scott." Her voice croaked and she looked away, blinking quickly.

He could still remember the way she looked, the last night they were together. It was one of those hot, sticky days in August. The kind of days that never seemed to end, and he never wanted them to—not when he was with Emily. They'd spent the day wandering through town, resting in the cool shade of the trees in the park, taking heat in each other's embrace and not even caring, so eager were they for the other's touch. Her long brown hair was damp at the forehead, pulled up in a ponytail, and he remembered the way he traced his fingers down the length of her neck, how her cheeks flushed from more than just the summer sun. He'd spent many days like this with her, but for some reason, on that day, he'd lingered at the edge of her porch, watching as she smiled to him from the top of the stairs, waiting until she was safely inside, and even then, wishing he could still cling to the sight of her for just a few more moments.

He'd clung to the image for years. The perky ponytail, the bright pink cheeks that made her gray eyes shine, and most of all, that smile. It was the smile of innocence, the smile of a girl who loved him completely, who trusted in him to never let her down. And he never wanted to.

"It was too hard to say goodbye," he said gruffly.

"Too *hard?*" Emily's eyes were steely and sharp, darkening to midnight as they locked his. "What was hard, Scott, was waking up one morning and discovering you were gone. And then waking up every morning after that wondering if it might be the day I heard from you again. And then realizing every night that I probably never would. That was hard."

Scott held her steady gaze, wanting more than anything to close the distance between their bodies, between the twelve years of disappointment he had caused her and the years of pain he had brought into her life. He wanted to take her into his arms and kiss the frown off her sweet mouth, to feel the curve of her waist under his hands, to make up for every tear he had ever caused her to shed.

He nodded, edging toward the door. She was right. Actions did speak louder than words. The way she saw it, he had led her on, made promises he had never intended to keep, and then never spoken to her again. She had no idea how far beyond that betrayal his actions had extended.

"Just tell me this much," she said. "Do you ever wonder how things might have been? If you'd stayed in town?"

He looked her square in the eye, grateful for a chance to be brutally honest. "Every day," he replied. Every damn day.

She nodded, but said nothing more.

"Have a good night, Emily," he said with a nod, his tone more clipped than he had intended. It was the only way to keep the conversation from continuing down a path that would only lead to more heartache. He needed to let her go. For the night. Maybe for good.

"See you."

See you. See you, she had called that evening, throwing him a casual smile, holding up a slender hand in a careless wave before turning her back and disappearing into the shadows of that old, run-down farmhouse she lived in with her mother and sister. Those were the last words she had ever said to him. If he'd known it then, he would have pressed for more, for an "I love you," a last kiss—something. But somehow, somewhere deep in his mind, in a nugget of hope that had no right to fight for life, he always found optimism in those two simple words: *See you.* It wasn't a goodbye. It wasn't the end. It was the promise of another encounter and perhaps, he'd sometimes dare to imagine, another chance.

He watched her for a long moment, his gaze lingering on the gentle flare of her hips, the way her long chestnut hair brushed against her shoulders. He hesitated, going so far as to even open his mouth— *Just tell her, tell her it was an accident, tell her how you feel!*—before he pulled his eyes from her for the night, knowing the image of her would stay with him until morning.

Her father was gone; her life had taken a new path in his absence. Nothing he could say to her now could make up for that. Nothing at all.

Emily was sitting on the couch reading a well-thumbed paperback, when her sister came out of her room. From her vantage point in the living room, she could see Julia's wide-eyed sweep of the small apartment. She tucked her head around the door frame and whispered, "Is he gone?"

Emily bit back a sigh. As if she didn't know. "You shouldn't have invited him inside," she scolded.

Julia's eyes flung open. "Are you kidding me? I told you, the two of you have unfinished business to address." She flopped onto a chair and tucked her feet under her, settling in for a long chat. "So tell me, what did he have to say for himself?"

Julia was watching her expectantly and Emily reluctantly dog-eared the page in her novel and set it in her lap. "Nothing. He said he had to go home."

Julia pinched her lips. "Figures."

"You didn't exactly help matters, Julia."

"Me?" Julia frowned. "You might be two years

older than me, but I am still your sister. You're all I've got. So if I want to say something to Scott, I will."

Emily closed her eyes, even though a part of her was touched by Julia's loyalty. It was a trait in her sister she had always admired—the ability to speak her mind and stand by her opinions, regardless of the consequence. Growing up, Emily had been the responsible one. The one who put dinner on the table when their mother worked late; the one who made sure Julia completed her homework each night. Julia was the tough one, though. The one who fought for what she believed in, who didn't take life passively. And Emily...well, Emily supposed she was always just grateful when something eventually worked out.

"I still can't believe you slammed that pie in his face," Julia said. "It's a start, at least."

Emily glanced toward the front door, thinking of Scott alone in that small room, and her heartstrings began to pull. She banished the thought, thinking instead of the man high-fiving Jack and Cole at the bakery, the man who was celebrated just for strutting back into town. The man who didn't have to take responsibility for the pain he left in his wake.

A giggle began to erupt in her as she replayed the memory of the afternoon. The astonishment in his eyes when she actually hit her target with that pie.

"What's so funny?" Julia asked, but a smile was already playing at her lips.

They laughed together, reliving the hilarious memory. Oh, the look on his face! She didn't know what had come over her to do such a thing, but oh, it had been worth it. Really, truly worth it.

"You're going to be laughing about this for a while,"

Julia said, shaking her head with a mischievous smile. She picked up her knitting needles and resumed where she had left off earlier. "Well, half the town will be talking about it by noon tomorrow."

"Julia…"

Julia flashed her a glance, her expression the picture of mock innocence. "What?"

Emily dipped her chin. "Don't go spreading gossip."

"Me? I'm insulted you would even suggest such a thing. I mean, I can't exactly help it if I have a knitting circle tomorrow morning, or if the expected topic of conversation will be the return of Scott Collins…"

Emily picked up her book and stood, stretching until her back arched. With a tired sigh, she regarded her sister and shook her head. "You missed your calling, my dear. You should have taken to the stage. You're all about drama. Especially when it's not your own."

She walked over to her sister, planted a kiss on her the top of her auburn hair and then padded off down the hall to her bedroom, unable to stop thinking of the fact that Scott Collins—the one man other than her father she had loved with all her heart her entire life—was somewhere on this floor, only a matter of twenty feet away from where she now sat, on the edge of her bed, staring out the window onto the quiet streets of Maple Woods.

She wondered if he was awake, or if the strange events of the night had exhausted him. She wondered if he was still thinking of her, of their conversation.

She wondered if in the past twelve years he had been gone, he had ever really thought of her at all. Or if that was just another one of his lies.

Chapter Four

It had rained overnight, a soft and pleasant tapping of drops against the windows accompanied by random bursts of lightning that lit the dark sky. The spring storm started at about midnight and went on until just past three, and Scott knew this because he was awake the entire time. Thinking about Emily.

He couldn't resist the relief he felt to know that Mrs. Porter had moved out of town, and that he wouldn't have to face her, too. She'd always been a kind woman, pleasant despite her circumstances, with a dullness in her soft gray eyes—the light having been replaced by sadness. For all the time that he and Emily had dated, her mother had always been off at one odd job or another, coming home harried and tired, but always with a smile on her face at the sight of her daughters. Mrs. Porter had always been kind to him, even as a child.

He remembered the time when he was riding his bike down Willow Road and hit a rock, she had run outside to help him, inviting him to come sit on her front porch while she cleaned and bandaged his scraped knees, offering him a glass of cool, sweet lemonade with a reassuring smile. "I don't have any sons," he remembered her saying with a wistful grin, "but I imagine you get into your share of trouble around here."

More trouble than she knew.

The memory of that hot summer afternoon made him feel queasy and restless, and he fitfully tossed and turned as the small room above the diner—just a mere twenty feet from Emily and Julia's apartment— illuminated with lightning, until the storm passed over and he finally fell into a disoriented sleep filled with nightmares, waking drenched in sweat only a few hours later.

The morning glow filtering through his window came as a welcome relief and by seven he was dressed and eager to escape the confines of his small room. He drove past the job site, surveying the damage to the historic town library. It was an accident, he knew: a stupid, careless incident that had resulted in serious structural damage of an entire wing of the building. He didn't blame Bobby. He hadn't done it on purpose. But could the same be said for Emily? Would she blame him?

Scott narrowed his eyes as he inspected the wreckage. Some accidents were pardonable. Others were permanent. They could never be put right.

He picked up a chunk of cement and tossed it back to the ground with a sigh. The crew couldn't start until they had plans in place, and with his father's condition

Scott knew it was up to him to lead the project or find a suitable replacement. He should go into the office and get started on this immediately, but he couldn't bring himself to do it. Not yet.

He shuddered when he thought back on those summers of his youth spent tagging along as his dad went about his work. He supposed it was ironic that he still pursued a career in the construction business, but maybe starting his own Pacific Northwest-based company was his way of taking back control of the events that had gone so awry in his past. Or maybe there were just some things in life you couldn't escape, no matter how hard you tried. The day Emily's father died was a fog—a disjointed stream of memories. But the one thing he could never forget were the shouts. The panicked, horrifying shouts. He'd just had no idea at the time that he was the one who had set it all into motion.

Scott straightened his back and marched to the car. His father had no problems covering up the truth, denying it. Well, not him. So many times over the years Scott had thought of picking up the phone and telling Emily the truth, but then he wondered if he would only hurt her more by setting himself free.

Scott drove into town and killed the engine at a spot in front of the diner. He needed a clear head before heading over to the office, and a Reuben sandwich with hot coffee would do just the trick.

"Scott!" The sound of his sister's voice across the room as he walked through the door pulled him out of his dark mood and Scott grinned back at her, moving eagerly through the crowded tables to grab the last stool at the counter. It seemed the room went quiet as he wove his path, but he refused to give in to it.

"What can I get for you?" Lucy asked with a smile. There was something in the crinkle of her eyes, an apology perhaps, an understanding. He closed his eyes briefly, showing his gratitude.

"A Reuben with extra fries," he said with a grin.

Lucy scribbled out a ticket and clipped it in line with the others. "Scott, this is Holly Tate. She runs The White Barn Inn down at the edge of town. Holly, this is the kid brother I've told you so much about."

"So you're the one who stuck a snake under Lucy's pillow?" Holly's lips curled into a sly grin, and Scott chuckled.

"The one and only." He extended his hand. "It's nice to meet you, Holly. I hope you won't judge me too harshly based on my mischievous past. I was only four when I captured that snake out at Willow Pond."

"Are you kidding? I love that story." Holly's laughter was soft and pleasant, and the warmth in her eyes helped his shoulders to relax. "I'm an only child myself. I would have killed for an annoying little brother."

"Hey, I'm the only one who's allowed to call my brother annoying," Lucy protested. She slid him a knowing glance as she filled his mug with coffee from a glass pot. "You were pretty annoying, but you turned out just fine."

Scott set his jaw and forced his attention back to Holly. "I don't think I remember you growing up in Maple Woods."

Holly shook her head. "I only spent the summers here so you might not have seen me. My grandmother lived here in the old white house I turned into the inn—"

"I know the one." Scott smiled at a fond memory of the stately old mansion and the kind woman who lived there. Studying Holly more closely, he had a vague recollection of a cute little granddaughter a couple years younger than himself.

Holly paused, her gaze becoming wistful. "I always loved Maple Woods. Once I inherited the house and moved back, I knew could never leave it."

Scott gave a noncommittal grunt. "It is a charming town," he managed. From the corner of his eye he could see Lucy watching him carefully. He fought to ignore her.

"My fiancé mentioned you were here to oversee the rebuilding of the library," Holly continued.

Scott nodded. The anonymous donor. According to Lucy, Max Hamilton had come into town with the intention to buy out the parcel of land housing the inn and turn it into a shopping mall. George's family owned the land, but had been leasing it to Holly's family for years. The opportunity to sell would allow them to pay to have the library rebuilt, but when Max fell in love with Holly and decided to stay in town and keep the inn running, Lucy was spared having to make the difficult decision of taking her friend's home out from under her in order to right her son's wrongs.

Scott swiveled in his seat to reach for his coffee, allowing the heat to coat his throat before he answered. "With our father unwell, Lucy asked me to take over the reins for a bit. I'm just in town to make sure all the projects on the books continue to run smoothly until a replacement can be found."

"I heard about your father," Holly said softly, darting her gaze to Lucy. "I'm sorry."

Scott shrugged but his stomach tightened. "Ah, well…" He lowered his eyes to his mug to avoid looking in Lucy's direction.

"So you're not going to oversee the library project, then?" Holly pressed. Her brow knit together. "I thought Max said you were."

Scott cursed to himself for being so careless with his words. He sensed her concern and he understood it—her fiancé was financing the project in exchange for George's land; they wanted to make sure the project would be built to their satisfaction. He knew he should just tell her the truth—that he would find a replacement, a project manager for the job, and that it wouldn't be him overseeing a minute of that project or any project having to do with his father's company—but for some reason, he couldn't. Not in front of Lucy. He couldn't let her down just yet. "I still have to get over to the office and sort through some things. We want to make sure the most qualified person oversees that job."

He scrolled through some work emails on his phone while Lucy began chatting with Holly about her various guests at the inn, and when his food arrived, he was grateful to have something positive to focus on. Within a few minutes, Holly left and Scott felt the heat of Lucy's gaze on him. There was a change in her expression, one he was familiar with; she had something on her mind. He took another bite of his sandwich, trying to avoid her stare.

Please don't talk about Dad. Not now. He knew he should offer her comfort, lessen the burden of the pain for her, share in the fear, but he didn't trust himself to speak. He'd been doing his damned best not to think about his parents since last night. He'd gone there for Lucy but he couldn't go back. He wouldn't.

"I'm sorry for the things I said last night," Lucy said.

Scott relaxed. "I know what you were trying to do. I'm just sorry you were disappointed with the outcome."

Lucy nodded, her lips thin. It was clear she had a lot more to say on the matter, but was refraining. "I could use a favor from you, if you don't mind picking up a hammer."

Well, this was a pleasant surprise. "You name it!" Scott said, smiling.

"The last of the cabinet doors for Sweetie Pie just arrived this morning. George is too busy to get to it this week, so I hoped you might be up for the job."

Scott stifled a frown. The prospect of yet another painful encounter with Emily didn't appeal to him. "Today?" he asked, his tone conveying his sudden shift in enthusiasm.

Lucy shrugged. "Or tomorrow." Her voice was pleasant and light but it was clear she wasn't going to let it drop.

"Isn't there someone else you could ask?" He asked before he could stop himself. Lucy's face had already folded in confusion and before she could say anything he blurted, "Don't worry. Of course I'll do it. In fact, I'll do it today, as soon as I'm done here."

Lucy regarded him, unconvinced. "If you're sure…"

Scott forced a grin. "You can always count on me, Lucy, and you know that. Now, where's the toolbox?"

He tried to tell himself it was a simple favor, and the least he could do for her after his outburst last night. After all, she didn't realize what she was asking of him. She didn't know what had happened to make him leave town and stay away—why he and their parents had severed all communication when he left. She wouldn't understand why Emily Porter was the last person in Maple Woods he had any desire to spend time with, much as he wished the circumstances were different.

Emily saw Scott coming across the street and felt the air lock in her chest. She quickly ran into the kitchen and fumbled in her handbag for a tube of lipstick, using the side of the toaster for a make-shift mirror. Frivolous nonsense! But she couldn't help herself—the image of that sheepish grin and apologetic shadow in his deep blue eyes made her hands shake, and she hastily swiped at her mouth to repair the damage. If only he wasn't so damn cute!

The chime of the bells above the door kick-started her pulse, despite her effort to remain calm. With one last deep breath, she squared her shoulders and sailed into the storefront before her nerves paralyzed her completely. If the way they'd left things last night was any indicator, today's forecast had awkward written all over it.

Scott stood behind the glass display case, idly perusing the pies. Smiling for courage, Emily said with forced cheer, "Back for more already?" *Maybe he's here to apologize,* she thought. To finish the conversation they'd started last night. Something told her she wasn't going to like what he had to say to her, though, and if he was going to let her down gently for something that had happened half a lifetime ago, then she'd rather be spared the further humiliation.

"My mouth says yes, but my stomach says no." He rubbed his rock-hard abdomen.

Even through his lightweight polo, Emily could make out the chiseled contours of his corded muscles. Heat pooled in her belly as she traced her eyes up the hard plane of his chest to the broad shoulders that filled his shirt, causing the material to go taut in all the right places.

"Actually, I'm at your service for once. Lucy asked me to install a couple of cabinet doors."

Well, that was interesting. Emily studied him through narrowed eyes.

She glanced around the shop to make sure no one needed her attention, but it was nearing two o'clock and there wouldn't be another surge of traffic until after dinner. "Sure, right this way."

Scott crossed behind the counter and she led him into the kitchen, a blush heating her cheeks at the awareness of his eyes on her. Her stomach tightened as she worried she might have somehow gotten some flour on the seat of her skirt when she'd leaned on the counter earlier. An uncomfortable silence hung heavy in her footsteps and she racked her brain for something to say to lighten the mood, or at least an excuse to get him to walk in front of her.

Finally, they were in the kitchen and she heard him place a toolbox down on the marble-topped island with a heavy thud before she came to a halt. Without daring to look at him, she stopped where a large flat box was propped against the wall.

"It arrived this morning. Back order," she explained, stealing a quick glance and then immediately looking away. She motioned to the empty space above the range. "Just up there, if you don't mind."

She caught another glimpse of his well-muscled form as he bent down to pop the box, her heart tightening with longing, recalling the way they used to be. The way he'd hold her hand when they walked home from school, the way he'd shout out to her when she sat in the stands, watching his football games, and the way she swelled with pride that he was hers and that he cared that she was there to cheer him on.

Yes, he'd *cared*. Once. She could still feel the sweetness of his first kiss that cool fall day of her freshman year—the gentle, almost hesitant way he had grazed her lips behind the old maple tree in the park next to their school. The way over time his body had become one with hers. She knew every contour, every slope—he was a constant in her life she had come to rely on, when she hadn't dared to take anything as a given since her father died. And then…poof! Gone.

She forced back the aching sensation in her chest. Did he have any idea how much he'd let her down? Did he even care?

From the looks of it, he didn't.

Without a word, Scott stepped closer and Emily felt her body warm on reflex. The musk of his aftershave caused her thoughts to revert to something primal and instinctive, stirring a part of her than had been dormant for too long. She shifted her eyes to her left, and dropped an arm as Scott reached up to take a measurement. He was absorbed in the task, his brow furrowing in concentration as he studied the small numbers.

Emily dared to regard him a little more closely, noticing the fine lines around his deep set eyes, the way his strong, chiseled jaw was laced with the faintest bit of stubble, the way his biceps flexed as he pulled the measuring tape taut.

She pulled her gaze away. She was only indulging in a fantasy by standing here, only wishing for things that could never be. Somehow she had thought when she was nearing thirty she would be more reasonable when it came to matters of the heart, that she would know how to reserve her feelings for a man who could return them, not run from them.

Leave it to Scott Collins to have her feeling like a teenager all over again.

"I'll get out of your way and let you work," she said, unfolding herself from his proximity.

She barely made it to the kitchen island when she heard his husky voice behind her. "Wait."

Her pulse lurched as she turned to face him. Was he going to explain? Finish the conversation they had started last night?

He stood where she had left him, arms at his sides, staring at her with an intensity that closed the gap between their bodies. She swallowed hard, her eyes locked with his. Did he regret the way things had left off last night? Or was he going to tell her he never loved her at all—that he was wrong to have ever let her believe otherwise? She didn't think she could bear it—in fact, she knew she couldn't—and suddenly she felt choked for air, dizzy with anticipation. She wanted to run out into the storefront, escape the magnificence of his raw, masculine energy and his heated gaze. She wanted to get on with life. Forget him. The way she should have forgotten him a long, long time ago.

"Mind passing me the flathead?"

Her eyes widened. After a pause, she clarified through a choked breath, "The flathead?"

His mouth twitched into a smirk. "The screwdriver."

Oh. So he just needed her help. She bit back a twinge of disappointment and the weight of it rested firmly in her gut. After a pause, she studied the contents of the toolbox impassively, aware of his watchful gaze as she searched for the specific tool. Finally, she plucked it from the box and handed it to him. "Here you go," she said in what she hoped was a breezy tone. The heat of the kitchen was beginning to feel stifling, and the penetrating gaze of Scott's misty blue eyes left her rattled and confused.

"This isn't the flathead," he said, flashing a set of straight, even teeth.

Her stomach tightened. "Oh." She paused and studied it in his hands. "It's not?"

"Nope." He strode by her and plunked it back in the box, swiftly retrieving another red-handled tool. "See the flat edge to the tip?" he asked, running his finger over the metal. "That's how it earned its name."

"Oh," Emily managed weakly. She shifted the weight on her feet, eager to get away from him, from those hooded blue eyes with their bright green flecks around the center. From the way they gleamed at her with a certain level of mischief that could only be born from intimacy.

Scott tipped his head toward the cabinet. "Do you have a few minutes to give me a hand?"

Emily glanced desperately through the kitchen doorway and into the empty bakery. There was no excuse she could give. "Sure," she said on a heavy sigh.

Scott pulled a chair over to the counter and stepped up, and Emily bit down on her lower lip as she gazed up at his form, mentally chastising herself for the ridiculous notions that began to spring to mind, unfiltered in their unabashed desire. She raked her eyes up the length of his legs, nearly groaning as she absorbed the curve of his hard thighs. She looked sharply away. She really needed to get out more. Or stop watching those damn soap operas!

Clenching her teeth, she handed him the screwdriver and watched him set the hinge. Something in his competent attitude elicited a swell of attraction deep within her, and she imagined what it must feel like to have a man in the home—a strong, capable, take-charge man. A man who could fix what was broken, and set things right. She was being silly and naive, she supposed, idealizing the missing piece in her life.

Her dad had died when she was only eight, but she still had the dollhouse he made for her for that last birthday he was with them, and she often admired the handiwork—the pride he took in the task. After he died, her mother had never remarried or even dated. She didn't have time, Emily reflected, thinking back on the two jobs her mother maintained to pay the bills. It was a fearful time, Emily recalled, and although her mother hid her grief and money concerns as best she could, Emily was old enough to be aware of their situation, and perceptive enough to know that she was helpless to make it much better.

Emily handed Scott the level he asked for and smiled sadly. If her dad were still alive, he would have probably built this whole kitchen himself. But then, if her dad were still alive a lot of things would have been different.

Scott opened and closed the cabinet door and smiled proudly at Emily, who stood below and granted him a small applause. "How about that?" he bantered, unable to resist flashing a grin at the beautiful woman whose company he just couldn't seem to get enough of, even if he was desperate to avoid her.

"Perfect," she said, sliding the chair back into place after he stepped down. "Lucy will be pleased. I know she's really glad you're back in town."

Scott loaded up the toolbox and closed it tight. Turning to face her, his eyes locked with hers and a shadow fell over her soft gray irises. *Just tell her. Tell her now. It's just you and her. Get it over with.* He cleared his throat. "Emily, I wanted to say—"

"If it's about last night, Scott, please...let's forget it." A flush had crept up her cheeks and she traced a path on the tile floor with the toe of her shoe.

"But that's just the thing, Emily. I can't forget it." *Any of it.* "Did you mean it when you said you moved on after I left?"

She looked up at him. "Would it matter if I had?"

He raised his eyebrows. "I suppose it wouldn't. If it made you happy."

Emily snorted. "Since when do you care if I'm happy, Scott?"

"Since always," he said firmly, searching her face. "You know how much I cared about you."

She held his stare, her lips growing thin. "No, I don't know that. I thought you did once, but then—"

"I'm sorry the way things ended between us, Emily. Please believe me when I say it because it's the truth."

"That's not exactly the way I remember things, Scott. The way I remember it, nothing ever ended with us, you just disappeared."

His jaw flinched. "I had my reasons," he said.

"Enlighten me." She tipped her head, locking her gaze on him.

He inhaled deeply, holding her stare, willing himself to let it out, to spill the truth. The horrible, awful truth. The minute hand ticked its way around the clock behind her. With a sigh of defeat he broke her gaze and shook his head. "Does it matter why? Can't it be enough that I'm sorry?"

She sighed, her eyes silently roaming his face. "You're really sorry? You really mean that?"

"More than you know," he insisted.

Emily paused with a hand on the counter. Finally she softly said, "You could have contacted me at some point. You could have told me what went wrong, why you left."

"It had nothing to do with you, Emily," he lied. He couldn't hurt her anymore. It was the last thing he wanted. He rubbed his forehead, his mind whirling with memories of that awful night when his parents told him the role he had played in her father's death so many years earlier, the night he realized that his entire life up until that point was an illusion, that he wasn't the person this town thought he was, that he could never be the man they wanted him to be. "It was this town, my parents. These...expectations!"

"I never expected anything from you, Scott," she said, searching his eyes. "All I ever expected from you was what you promised me."

He grimaced at her words. "I wanted to fulfill those promises, Emily. I just…" He shook his head. "I was too young to know how to handle it."

The expression in her eyes went flat. "It wasn't the time for us, I guess."

"I guess not," he managed.

Silence fell over the kitchen. In the distance, he could hear the old church bell toll the hour. He remembered how much Emily loved that sound. She used to tell him it gave her a feeling of hope, a feeling of anticipation that something wonderful was happening. He'd told her she was being romantic, caught up in fantasies about wedding days and white dresses, but inwardly he was charmed by the simple pleasures she found in life.

"What are you smiling about?" she asked now.

"Do you remember the time you told your mother we were going to be studying all day in the library for a big test and we drove to New York instead? Made it less than two hours, too."

"You always drove too fast." Emily laughed. "That was the worst lie I ever told and I still feel bad about it."

Scott felt his gut stir. Determined to cling to something good, he pressed, "I remember you came with me to the top of the Empire State Building, even though you were always afraid of heights."

"I still am." Emily's lips twisted into a smile. "I knew how much you wanted to go up, though. And I didn't want to miss a moment of the day with you."

"After that, you insisted I keep your feet on the ground." He grinned as the details of that day came clearer. He hadn't thought of it in a long time. "I took you to Central Park."

"You set up that picnic for us, even though it was freezing outside. My hands were shaking so hard, I spilled my coffee all over the blanket." She smiled.

"Hey, I thought I was being romantic!" he said, but he was laughing now, too. He would do it all differently if he took Emily back to the city again. He'd do a lot of things differently.

She tipped her head. "You were romantic," she said lightly, but a shadow crossed over her face. "You were…very sweet."

His chest tightened. "We had a lot of good times together, Em."

She smiled sadly. "We did."

Scott took a step back. He didn't trust himself around her. Her full, pink lips were slightly parted, and an irrational and all-consuming urge to step forward and claim her mouth with his erupted in him. But as always, his desire for her was drowned with guilt.

In a perfect world he and Emily might have had something, but he had learned a long time ago that the world was cruel and she of all people probably shared the thought.

"Emily—" he started, and then stopped. Without thinking, without processing his actions, he had reached over and placed his hand on hers, as naturally as he had a thousand times before. She stiffened under his touch, her gaze widening as she glanced down to his hand, and he knew he should release it. He should let her go the way he intended to all those years ago. But he couldn't, damn it. He couldn't.

He wrapped his fingers around hers, watching the soft rise and fall of her shoulders, the way her lashes fluttered. Her hand felt small in his, exactly as it always had, and he realized in that moment that no matter what had changed, some things still hadn't. She was still the girl he'd always loved.

"I should probably get going," he said, releasing her and backing away. He smiled as she lifted her gaze to his. "It's been nice talking to you, though, Emily. Really nice."

There was a lingering sadness in her eyes. "You too, Scott."

He hesitated, wishing he could reach out and take her hand again, pull her close and kiss her lips and feel her body close to his.

He turned on his heel, inhaling sharply. No good would come of that. No good at all. He had caused Emily enough grief to last a lifetime; he didn't need to think about breaking her heart again while he was at it.

Chapter Five

Emily heard the tread of Scott's footsteps on the stairs at about half past six. She'd been waiting for his arrival with bated breath since her shift ended at four, and now she tilted her head and strained her ear as she mentally followed his path. His stride remained even as he approached her door and passed it.

She checked her watch. It was Wednesday, which meant Julia would be indisposed at the yarn shop with the weekly open project knitting group. Emily usually looked forward to Wednesday nights—it was a chance to see her friends Holly Tate and Abby Webster from The White Barn Inn, as well as a few of the other women from town—but tonight she had more important things on her mind than finishing the merino wool cowl she wouldn't wear until October or catching up on the latest gossip in town or over at Holly's inn.

She popped into the bathroom and regarded herself in the mirror. Carefully, she applied an extra touch of blush to her cheeks and took a brush to her long, thick hair. Better. She inhaled deeply, checked her reflection from a few more angles, flicked off the light as she tiptoed into the kitchen, and then stopped. Why was she was sneaking around her own apartment like a cat burglar?

She shook her head at her folly. The truth was that since learning Scott was staying only one door down the hall, her heart had been permanently filled with anticipation. For what, she chastised herself, the odd chance he came knocking at three in the morning to profess his undying love?

Life just didn't work that way. Much as she wished it did.

Still, she wasn't ready to give up on him just yet. She knew he had been as surprised as she was when he'd taken her hand today. She'd seen that glimmer of shock—and heat—pass through his eyes. But he hadn't snatched his hand back, hadn't made up an excuse at all. Instead, he'd let it stay there, the weight of it on hers reminding her of the closeness they had once shared, making her long for him in places deep inside herself, places she had forgotten even existed.

She shivered now, recalling his touch. No, she couldn't give up just yet. Something about the softness in his voice when he apologized gave her reason to hesitate. He'd sounded so sincere. Maybe there was more reason to his departure than he'd let on. If so, she was determined to get to the bottom of it.

Emily picked up the fresh cherry pie that was cooling on the counter and bent down to inhale its sweet aroma. Perfect. Listening for any further sounds of life in the building, Emily carefully unlatched the door and padded quietly down to the end of the hall. Her knuckles felt tentative against the smooth grain of Scott's door, and she chewed her lip, wondering if she should try again—more assertively this time—when the door swung open and Scott's inquisitive gaze met her eyes.

Well, you've done it now, Em. Keep going, girl. You can't exactly turn and run...

She tipped her head and curved her lips into a smile, willing her voice not to quiver. "Thought I'd thank you for helping with the cabinet today," she said, extending hands that were holding the pie swaddled in a crisp cotton tea cloth. It had seemed like such a good idea two hours ago, and now watching Scott's sea-blue gaze roam from her face to the oozing pie in her hands, she began to waver. "It's cherry," she added, even though that much was glaringly oblivious.

Scott's lips twitched into a grin. "Should I grab a towel? Start running the shower?"

She laughed—louder than she had planned as the nerves found release. "Don't worry. I think my pie tossing days are behind me."

"I have to admit you have a better arm than I remembered." He flashed a megawatt smile and pulled the door wide. "Want to come in?"

Emily feigned hesitation and then said with a forced shrug, "Um...sure. Why not?"

She stepped over the threshold and swept her eyes over the room, from the perfectly made bed to the small kitchenette to the en suite bathroom to the open suitcase, still packed and ready. He certainly hadn't made himself at home, she observed.

Her heart sank. He really wasn't planning on sticking around for long.

"I had been thinking of stopping by your place later, actually," he said, watching her carefully, and her heart skipped a beat.

"Oh?"

He cast her a crooked grin. The sudden boyish quality to his expression took her back twelve years, to the time and place when he'd captured her heart. She could still feel the lurch of her pulse when he took her in his arms... If she closed her eyes she could still smell the damp heat of his skin, the musk of his hair. The way his soft lips had—

"I wasn't sure it was such a good idea, though," he continued. A shadow crept over his rugged features.

"Couldn't bear to face the wrath of Julia?" Emily lifted a brow as she met his gaze and they both slipped into easier smiles. "She was a little hard on you last night," she admitted.

Scott shrugged. "She had her reasons." His jaw set. "I had it coming anyway."

He caught her eye and her breath hitched. She swallowed hard, forcing herself to remember the way they had left things this afternoon, the memories they shared and treasured. "Some things are best forgotten," she said lightly, wondering if she was convincing him of this any better than herself.

She stared at the still-packed suitcase, open on the top of the dresser. Memories or no memories, she and Scott weren't meant to be. Not then. Not now. Not ever. Why couldn't she just accept it once and for all?

"First love isn't easily forgotten," Scott replied, his voice so low she barely heard him. She glanced up to him, noticing the way he stared pensively out the window. He turned to her suddenly, his smile sad, his eyes still distant and focused on something beyond this room. "I know I never forgot you, Emily."

Scott led Emily to the drop-leaf table near the window, sliding over two chairs, then handed her a plate. It was either that or the bed, and something told him that inviting Emily to sit there was more than his self-control could handle right now. As it was, he barely trusted himself to be alone in this small room with her at all. There was too much bubbling below the surface, screaming for release. He was torn between blurting out the dark, hidden secrets or reaching across the table and pulling her into his arms. He wanted to taste her lips, explore her mouth and feel the swell of her breasts against his chest. He wanted to run his fingers through her hair and trace the length of her neck with his kisses until she shivered under his touch.

He gritted his teeth. Obviously, none of those were options at the moment.

"You're very talented, you know," he said as he sank his fork into the pie. "Have you ever thought about pursuing your culinary skills?"

Emily's brow seemed to furrow slightly at the question, but she recovered quickly. "Well, I work at Sweetie Pie," she pointed out.

Scott nodded. "True. I guess I just meant something of your own. With your talent…well, there must be something you could do with it."

As he met her bewildered expression, his heart tensed with regret. Damn, he couldn't do anything right with Emily!

"Well, I didn't have the means to go to college, and my mother needed my help here," Emily said, and Scott felt the evidence of his shame heat his neck. "But then, you knew that."

"I didn't mean to upset you," he protested, his eyes searching the small oak table for retribution. "I honestly meant it as a compliment."

Emily offered him a slow grin. Scott shifted uncomfortably on the stiff wooden chair to ward off his growing attraction.

"Don't worry," she said easily. She lifted her chin and chewed thoughtfully. "If I didn't know better, I might think I make you nervous."

A scoff released from his lips, but he didn't bother to deny it. He'd done enough lying for one lifetime. "Would that be so hard to believe?"

"As a matter of fact, it would."

"Well, you do make me a little nervous," he admitted with a wink.

Emily guffawed, but her eyes shone with interest. "Since when?"

Scott shrugged. "Since always. You were…special." He held her eyes from the hood of his brow. "I guess that's why you meant so much to me."

Her mouth thinned. "Not enough," she said matter-of-factly, glancing down at her plate.

It was the moment he had waited for, alone with her, calm, simple. He wanted to tell her the truth and shield her from it all at once. "I know you still don't believe me," he said, swallowing hard. "I did love you, Emily."

Her brow furrowed. "You sure had a weird way of showing it," she said, but he could hear the pain scratch through her voice. He could take the confusion away in one simple sentence. Give her the reason she craved for why he'd left so suddenly. But doing so…

He couldn't do it. He'd lost her once. If she knew, she'd be gone forever. He didn't think he could face that. Not yet.

"Young and dumb." He forced a casual tone, smiling tightly. He held her eyes with his, watching the light flicker through her wide black pupils. "Guess some things aren't meant to be."

"Guess not."

Silence stretched in the room, and Scott forked off a piece of the crumbling crust. When he'd cleaned his plate, he cut another thick slice, noticing Emily's watchful eye across the table. "Sorry, couldn't resist," he said with a grin.

She smiled. "Enjoy. The leftovers are yours. If there are any," she added, and then started giggling into her napkin.

Scott chuckled and broke through the lattice crust with his fork. "I don't know how you keep your figure working in that place," he said, dragging his eyes over her slim shoulders and taught waist.

"If you're trying to butter me up, you don't have to go that far," she said, but a flush had crept over her soft porcelain cheeks.

Scott leaned across the table. "It's Julia I really need to worry about kissing up to now, isn't it?"

Emily gave him a sly grin. "I think she's had her say and now she'll let it drop."

Scott watched her, unconvinced. "I'm not so sure." Emily's sister had always been a spitfire, even when she was younger. He could still remember the time he'd had to bribe Julia to keep quiet with a bag of candy after she'd spotted him through parted curtains giving Emily a good-night kiss on the front porch. Looking back, he almost chuckled aloud. Emily's mother wouldn't have minded. It was his parents who had never supported the relationship.

Emily waved her hand through the air. "Oh, don't worry about Julia. She might never admit it, but deep down I think she's tickled pink you're staying down the hall. It's the most exciting thing that's happened to her outside of *Passion's Crest.*"

Scott sputtered and coughed into his hand. *"Passion's Crest?"* he repeated.

A pink blush stained Emily's cheeks. "It's a soap opera. Julia's, um, rather caught up with it."

Scott's lips twitched with amusement. "I see."

"So, don't let her scare you off," she added hurriedly. "She can take a bit of drama."

Scott considered the meaning behind her words. She didn't want him to stay away, he realized. He sat back in his chair, watching her pick at the crumbs on her plate with the tip of her fork. "I'd really like to move forward, Emily," he said. "I never felt right about the way things ended. I...I want to make things right for you while I'm here in town." He forced a grin, wondering if his tone betrayed his inner concern. "Think you can forgive me?"

Emily's eyes roamed his face quietly. "You seem to feel really guilty," she pondered aloud.

"More than you know." He swallowed the last of the pie, tasting nothing.

Interest flickered in her gaze. After a pause, she tipped her head and smiled pleasantly. "I can see that cherry pie is still your favorite," she commented, motioning to his empty plate.

"And on that note, I think I'll take seconds." As he cut into the pie once more, he stopped himself, and slid her a glance. "I mean...thirds," he said, grinning.

"Comfort food," her voice came softly.

"When I was younger, my family and I always looked forward to a homemade pie. It seemed to always make things just a little brighter."

His stomach burned and he attempted to numb the pain with a hearty bite. If he kept going like this, he'd lose the physique he'd achieved by spending an hour in the gym each morning. Right now, he honestly didn't care.

"You remember how tight money was for my family after my father died." She paused, and drew a deep breath. "My mom was working two or three jobs at times and couldn't always make it home for dinner, but Sunday she was always at home, and we looked forward to that night all week, because that's when she made pie."

It was a sweet story, nearly pleasant enough to make him forget the horrible part he had played in her young life. It gave him some hope to learn that there were glimmers of happiness in her childhood after all. "She baked every Sunday?"

"Every Sunday." She smiled at the memory. Catching his stare, she smiled and shrugged. "Guess I associate pies with a feeling of comfort and safety. Sounds silly, I know."

Scott swallowed hard, his gaze lingering on the fullness of her mouth, the slender frame of her shoulders as she hunched over her plate. "I don't think it's silly at all."

He cleared his throat. "My family could have learned a lot from yours. My dad was always at work and when we did eat together, there was no real laughter, no warmth."

"Guess I should be happy you never brought me over for dinner, then," Emily said, but through her smile Scott could sense the twinge of hurt and confusion.

He pressed his lips together, thinking of how cold his father had always been to Emily, how his mother would casually change the subject when Scott mentioned her. He'd asked to bring Emily to dinner once in the entire three years they dated, and his father had made it clear that she wasn't welcome. At the time, he'd attributed it to snobbery on his parents' part. Collins was a big name in town, an established name, and Emily was one of...*Those poor Porters.*

"My family wasn't like yours, Em. You know that. You all had something. Love, joy. You knew each other."

Emily tipped her head. "You didn't know your parents?"

"Not one bit."

Emily studied him thoughtfully. "I remember the time your father saw us walking down Main Street, holding hands." She shook her head at the memory. "I swear, he turned white as a ghost."

Scott scowled. "He barely said hello to us. Typical."

"Well, Lucy's been like the big sister I never had." She gave him a wan smile.

Scott nodded. "Lucy's great. But my parents… It was a reflection of them, not you, Emily."

A shadow darkened her gray eyes. "I've been meaning to tell you that I was sorry to hear about your father's condition."

Scott stiffened, sobered by the shift in topic. "Thanks."

"If you ever wanted to talk about it, I'm around." She hesitated. "I…I understand." Her eyes pleaded with his in a knowing connection.

"I appreciate that," he said tightly. He hated that everyone in town knew why he was back. His father was dying; he couldn't deny it any more than he could hide from it. It was a fact, and in a small town like Maple Woods, the truth had a way of seeping out and spreading like thick molasses. He grimaced to think of the secret he had only managed to harbor by leaving town all those years ago.

Nausea rose in his stomach as he sat in Emily's presence. Even after everything he had done to her, she was still standing here, offering to be his friend. And he needed a friend, damn it. He needed a friend now more than ever.

The problem was that he wanted a hell of a lot more than friendship from Emily. He wanted everything he knew she could have given him if things had been different. But relationships couldn't be founded on lies, and in twelve years he still hadn't found a way to explain himself to her.

"It's hard to lose a father," she commented, her eyes once again warming with understanding and all at once Scott knew this was a bad idea. He shouldn't be near her.

Shame bit at him, and he didn't trust himself to speak. If he did, he might tell her everything just to set himself free of the weight that he had carried with him for so long. Every word he spoke to her felt like a lie, but the truth was too unbearable to say aloud.

His hand inched across the table. Searching her soft gaze, he saw a kindness there that tugged at his chest. She was compassionate, sweet, but everyone had their limits.

She was watching him closely, her expression so pure, her eyes so trusting and sure, that he had to snatch his hand back before he did something he would later regret.

Finishing her last bite of crust, Emily's lips twisted with mischief as she eyed the pie. "Since you've had thirds, I suppose I may as well have seconds...."

"You don't want me eating alone." Scott smiled.

"No, that would be rude...."

"And it would give you a reason to stay and chat a little longer—"

A shadow crossed over Emily's face but when her lips curled into a slow smile, his heart soared. "I'd like that. I'd like that very much, actually."

Not tonight, he decided as he placed another slice of pie on her plate. Tonight wasn't the night to make up for the sins of his past. Tonight he was simply going to enjoy the present.

Julia was already home by the time Emily turned the key in the door, and she forced a sober expression as she stepped into the kitchen, where her sister was preparing a pot of tea.

"Want a cup?" Julia asked, barely sparing her a glance.

"I'd love one." Emily slipped off her sandals while Julia stacked the teapot, two mugs and a plate of cookies on an old wooden tray and then followed her into the living room.

"You're getting home late tonight," Julia observed, carefully setting the tray on the coffee table—it rattled precariously from the weight and Emily reached out a hand to steady it. "Thanks." Her sister settled back into the sofa and pulled a chenille throw on top of her pajama-clad legs. While the day had been warm with sunshine, a cool spring breeze filtered in through the cracked window. "If Lucy keeps working you this hard, you're going to need to plan for early retirement."

Emily smiled benignly and reached for the remote control. "I wonder what drama unfolded today," she mused aloud, her tone ominous but laced with mock excitement. It didn't feel good to skirt Julia's comments. Her sister thought she was being worked to the bone, when really she had been enjoying a pleasant evening with Scott. There was plenty she would love to share, and she was sure that Julia would be thrilled to glean further insight into the elusive Scott Collins, but for some reason, she wasn't ready for the spell to be broken just yet. It would seem like a betrayal in a way, to sit here talking about Scott when he was only twenty feet down the hall from where she sat. Besides, something about keeping the details of her visit with him to herself made it feel more special. Once she opened up to Julia, there was no telling what type of speculation and doubts her sister would inadvertently stir up. Not that there was anything to speculate about.

Emily pinched her lips and glanced sidelong at her sister. Beside her, Julia was happily munching on a cookie, her eyes wide as the opening credits of *Passion's Crest* rolled. It was then that Emily realized she hadn't even checked the mail yet today, and that for some reason she didn't really want to. For today at least, she had everything she wanted right here in Maple Woods: a job she loved, her sister and the man she had loved for as long as she could remember.

As she stirred two lumps of sugar into her tea and cupped it in her hands, her stomach began to stir uneasily. She tried to force her concentration on the television and the gripping ups and downs of her favorite characters, but it was no use.

"Emily? Emily?" Startled, Emily turned to see Julia motioning to the remote next to Emily. "Are you going to fast forward through the commercials or make me sit here stuffing my face while I wait for the next scene?" She held up a cookie to drive her complaint home.

Emily chuckled, picked up the remote and did as she was told.

"I thought I smelled a pie when I walked in here tonight," Julia said casually a few seconds later, her eyes shining. Emily looked away as her sister continued, "Since you weren't at the bakery when I passed by, I thought maybe you had made some dessert for us tonight." She held her gaze steady, her expression blank. "Guess I wasn't the lucky recipient."

A heavy pause fell over the room and Emily bit back a wave of frustration laced with amusement. Pursing her lips, she paused the screen just after the last commercial of the set and placed the remote control on the coffee table so she could give Julia her full attention. "If you knew I wasn't at the bakery tonight, why did you make that comment when I came in the door?"

Julia shrugged and her lips curled with mischief. "It seemed easier than asking what the view is like from Scott's window."

Emily's eyes flung open. After the shock had left her, she tossed her head back in laughter. "I can't get anything past you," she said ruefully, wagging a playful finger at her sister's triumphant expression. "How'd you guess?"

"*Guess?* I heard." Julia arched a brow. "The walls here are very thin, you know," she said pointedly.

Discomfort tightened Emily's chest at the thought of Scott still so close by. Lowering her voice and hoping Julia would follow her lead, she confessed, "Fine. I stopped by Scott's room this evening."

Julia's grin lingered. "How'd that go?"

Emily shrugged. "Fine, I guess."

"Doesn't sound just fine to me."

Emily sighed. She leaned back against the couch and blew on the steam rising up from her mug. "The truth is that it doesn't matter how things went, Julia. The guy's only passing through town. He's made it very clear he doesn't want to stay any longer than he has to."

"Unless he can be convinced otherwise."

"Please," she said, but despite her protestation, Emily couldn't help but feel her hope becoming somewhat restored by Julia's words. She pushed the thought aside immediately and locked her sister's eyes. "This isn't like our soap opera, Julia. This is Maple Woods, not *Passion's Crest.* I'm not Marlene and Scott isn't Rafe Turner. I can't stir up some drama and twist things around to keep him here. Real life doesn't work that way."

Julia just tipped her head mildly, and said, "If that's how you want it to be."

"What's that supposed to mean?" Emily shot back.

"Seems to me that you sat back and let Scott walk away from you all those years ago. And now you're about to do it all over again."

Emily's temper flared. "That's not fair."

"Isn't it? What Scott did to you was wrong, there's no doubt about it, but I don't remember you asking for his whereabouts, demanding an explanation or trying to understand why things didn't work out. Seems to me you made it pretty easy for him then, and you're making it just as easy now."

Emily's chest was heavy with the pounding of her heart and she set the cup of steaming tea down before her shaking hands caused it to spill. She turned to glare at her sister. "What do you suggest then, Julia? Last I checked, you were up in arms about the way Scott treated me, and you made sure he knew it last night, too. Why the sudden change of heart?"

"Scott's no angel, but you like him and you always have. You've never been good at opening your heart since Daddy died. Then when Scott let you down…"

"This isn't about Dad," Emily said sharply.

Julia stared at her, unconvinced. "I just think that if you want something enough, you have to go after it. Take the risk."

Unbelievable. "And going over there tonight wasn't a risk?" The pitch in her voice caused Emily to wince.

Julia paused. "I just don't want to see you spend the next twelve years the way you've spent the last, that's all."

Oh, believe me, Emily thought with newfound resolve, *I don't plan to.*

She stood and handed the remote control to Julia, ignoring her younger sister's pleas to sit back down. "But we still don't know if Brad's the father!" she protested.

Lifting her chin, Emily excused herself to bed, denying the little part of her that really did want to know who had fathered Fleur's baby—Brad, or his evil twin brother, Chad? The suspense was killing her, but she thickened her determination. It could wait.

As she passed by the stack of mail Julia must have brought in with her, she glanced through the contents halfheartedly—nope, nothing for her except bills— and then wandered back to her bedroom. The week had caught up with her, but it would not keep her awake. No, tonight she would dream, but not of girlish hopes or unfilled dreams. Tonight she would dream of the future. The one she could control and make her own. Even if Scott would never be a part of it.

Chapter Six

Julia's words still haunted Emily the next morning as she walked down Main Street, holding an umbrella over her head as shelter from the morning drizzle. Leave it to her sister to voice every sinking sensation she had tried desperately to ignore for so many years of her life. Sometimes it was easier to put your head in the sand and keep going than to the face the truth. Even about yourself.

The soft glow illuminating from the Sweetie Pie Bakery was warm and inviting on this dreary day, and despite her equally drab mood, Emily felt herself perk up as she opened the door and stepped inside. The sweet scents of butter and sugar teased her as she shook out her umbrella. "Hello!" she called out.

"In the kitchen!" cried back Lucy's familiar voice.

Emily propped her umbrella in the stand near the

door and wiped her feet on the mat before heading back to the kitchen. Lucy's face was flushed, her eyes bright, and Emily immediately noted it wasn't from the heat of the oven.

"Is everything okay?" she asked gently, tilting her head in concern.

Lucy blinked a few times and managed a watery smile. "Sorry about this. It's just…" She inhaled sharply, unable to finish her sentence.

Slowly, Emily retrieved her apron from the hook on the door, taking time in tying it around her waist. Lucy and Scott had always had a complicated relationship with their parents from what Emily knew, but that didn't mean they didn't love them. Mr. and Mrs. Collins rarely ever came into the diner or town, but the few times they did, Emily couldn't help but notice the way Lucy fluttered around nervously, clearly hoping to meet her parents' approval. She wanted them to be proud of her, even if she hadn't chosen the path they had wanted for her.

"I stopped by my parents' house last night to drop off a casserole," Lucy explained, her back to Emily as she carefully set a pie on a cake pedestal. "My dad looked even worse than the night before."

"I'm so sorry to hear that." Despite the hard edge to Mr. Collins and the standoffish, cold nature of his wife, Emily couldn't wish any sorrow onto her friend. Or Scott.

"I'm afraid there might not be much time," Lucy continued, and Emily frowned. "All the better that Scott came back when he did, though I'm not sure what good it's done." She hesitated, rubbing her brow. "At least I can know I tried."

Emily nodded slowly, working up the courage to ask the burning question she had harbored for so long. It was one of Maple Woods's greatest mysteries. "Why do you think he stayed away so long?"

Lucy shrugged heavily and shook her head. "Oh, who knows really." She sighed, whisking some chocolate mousse. "I was out of the house and married with a kid when Scottie left. All I know is that he and my parents got in some huge fight that summer after he graduated from high school. I thought going off to college would help him calm down, let things blow over on both sides, but the distance only seemed to become permanent then. And he never came back."

Emily narrowed her eyes in concentration as she added some heavy cream to a stainless steel bowl and whisked in a few teaspoons of confectioners' sugar. She tried to connect the events, but to her frustration, she couldn't make sense of them.

As the cream began to hold peaks, she mused, "Did your parents ever tell you what the disagreement was about?" Deep down she'd always assumed it was about her. Though Scott had never said it, she'd known his parents hadn't approved of their relationship. They'd wanted him to go to college and take over the family company. Not marry a girl whose father had used to work for them.

"No, never." Lucy stopped stirring as a shadow crept over her face. "It was strange, actually. I tried to talk to them about it at first, but the more I pressed, the more firm they grew in their insistence that I stay out of it. I was so stunned by the intensity of their reaction that I never directly approached Scott about it, either."

"And he never opened up?"

Lucy shook her head. "Nope. I always gently encouraged him to come home—God knows how much I missed him and wanted him back. Each time he turned down the suggestion, I knew that was my answer. He wasn't ready. He hadn't gotten over whatever had happened between him and our parents."

"Do you think he has now?"

Lucy's brow pinched and she huffed, "No. I don't. I had to practically beg him to come back to town and when he came to the house the other night, it was very clear he wasn't ready to forgive them. A dying man, can you imagine?" Her eyes flashed on Emily's, and Emily, startled, stopped whisking the cream. This was very odd, indeed.

"What did he say?" she murmured, trying to imagine the scene.

Lucy threw up her hands and a dollop of chocolate mousse splattered against a wall. "I couldn't hear. It was muffled through the door and the next thing I knew Scott came flying down the stairs, telling me that I never should have made him come back, that it had just made everything worse." She sighed, and Emily noticed her hand was trembling as she reached for a dishrag. "Maybe he was right."

"He loves you," Emily said, and Lucy granted her a brave smile.

"In his own way," Lucy said with a bob of her head.

"How were your parents afterward?" Emily asked carefully, sensing Lucy was on the verge of tears.

Lucy considered the question. "I don't think they were surprised," she said simply. She turned to the oven and bent down to check on the status of a meringue.

A tight knot formed in Emily's stomach and she set her whisk down on the counter, staring into the thick peaks of whipped cream. If Scott couldn't even handle being in town after all this time, what made her think he would even consider staying in Maple Woods a day longer than he had to?

All the more reason to get out of town herself, she decided, her mouth thinning to a grim line as she began crushing chocolate cookies for the crust with the back of a rolling pin. Today's special was Chocolate Truffle and so help her, she would pound her emotions out on the cookie crust if it took all day.

The phone trilled and Lucy walked over to the counter to answer it. Emily bit back the wave of disappointment that their conversation had been interrupted. All for the better, she knew deep down. The more she thought about Scott, talked about Scott, schemed about Scott, dreamed about Scott, spent time with Scott…well, the bigger this rut would get. It was time to start living her own life and stop worrying about what Scott did with his. He had chosen his own path for reasons she might never understand but would simply have to accept.

From behind the wall, Lucy murmured a few words and then set down the receiver. "They're short staffed at the diner," she explained. And then, before Emily could comment, her expression collapsed. "I don't think I can handle going over there today," she admitted, her eyes pleading.

Emily searched her friend's face in bewilderment. "Of course not," she said, realizing that Lucy's Place required too much energy and pep when you were feeling as low as Lucy was this morning. She set down her rolling pin. "Why don't I cover the diner today and you can stay put? It's quieter here, and baking is therapeutic."

Lucy managed a smile and placed a hand on Emily's arm in affection. "Thank you." The intensity of her tone struck Emily and she frowned as she wordlessly untied her apron and placed it back on the hook. The diner was one of Lucy's favorite places to be—she usually loved chatting with the regulars that stopped in. If the thought of going there was this unbearable, then things with Mr. Collins must be very bad indeed.

How, then, could Scott still be so hardened to it all?

It was nearly eleven o'clock by the time Scott looked up from the pile of papers he'd been studying all morning. The large, polished mahogany desk in his father's office was strewn with blueprints and spreadsheets. Scott had been staring at them for hours, and he still didn't feel any closer to knowing how best to handle the information in front of him.

Collins Construction had been around for generations, serving as one of the largest businesses in Maple Woods, and it had always been a sound and financially secure company—his father had made sure of that, Scott thought bitterly. Judging from the books, business was now at a standstill, and the company had downsized in the past twelve years, resulting in two sets of layoffs already. Scott knew that the local economy hadn't been strong, and of course there was only so much building a town like Maple Woods required, but the surrounding towns that had once called on Collins Construction to bid seemed to be opting for larger, more modern companies, and the only project even scheduled was the rebuilding of the town library.

Scott reached into his pocket and pulled out a tube of antacids. Popping one into his mouth, he couldn't help but reflect on the irony of the situation before him. This was exactly the situation his father had wanted to avoid—financial ruin of his beloved company. Everything he had done—or failed to do—had been in a vain effort to avoid this exact scenario.

What a waste.

As darkening thoughts encroached, Scott rolled up the blueprints and tucked some papers into a file folder, opting to take the back door to his car to avoid any potential exchange with the staff. The last thing he needed was someone inquiring about the health of his father, or wanting to engage in a conversation about how it felt to be back in town after all this time. It felt lousy. And confusing as hell. But try telling them that.

He grinned wryly as he imagined the shock of his father's white-haired assistant if he gave her such a retort, and with a newfound smile on his face, he slipped into the red convertible and revved the engine. The familiar sound eased his mind, reminding him of the life he had waiting for him back in Seattle.

Even if it was a lonely life.

The drive to town was short—less than eight minutes—and he forced his attention on the road as he drove down Main Street, doing his best to ignore the ogling from the townsfolk strolling past. Let them think what they would. They'd probably already come up with some tantalizing speculation for what had kept him away and what had brought him back. He smiled grimly. Their wildest imaginations would never beat reality.

Or so he hoped.

After parking the car in a spot behind the diner, he pulled open the door of the establishment and glanced around. In a brief phone call with Max Hamilton that morning, they'd agreed to meet at noon, but he hadn't thought to ask for a description. He'd assumed he'd notice an unfamiliar face, but his recollection of the locals had faded. He struggled to remember names, and a dozen years had turned old neighbors into strangers. He swept his eyes to the back of the room, interest causing his pulse to take speed as he spotted Emily cheerfully chatting with a customer. The man was laughing at something she was saying, and he reached out and patted her hand in a friendly way. Too friendly, Scott thought, frowning.

"Emily. Hi." His abrupt tone forced her attention from the other man and Emily's sharp gaze darted to his, brightening as he closed the distance between them. He broke her stare to size up the man who was casually sitting on the barstool as if he owned the place. The man's familiarity with Lucy's diner and with Emily unnerved him, and he clenched his teeth at the sudden disadvantage.

Regret, he realized, owning the emotion. But then, neither his sister nor Emily were his to be so possessive over. He'd given up that right twelve years ago.

"I don't think we've met." He stared grim-faced at the man beside him, disturbed by the easy grin his opponent wore.

"Max Hamilton," the man said, extending a hand.

His shoulders relaxed. "Scott Collins," he said. He gave a firm shake. "Good to meet you."

"Emily and I were just talking about the Spring Fling this Saturday," Max explained. "Apparently they need a few volunteers for the pie-eating contest."

"You up for the challenge?" Emily asked from across the counter. She shared a grin with Max, clearly a good friend, and then drifted her gaze suggestively to Scott.

"I think I've had enough of pie contests for one week," he bantered, and Emily's cheeks grew pink.

"Ah, yes," Max chuckled. "I heard you stood in for the mayor this week. Made you a bit of a town hero, from what I gathered."

Some town hero all right. Even after his disappearing act, somehow he was still the football champ in the eyes of the locals. Still the kid who had put Maple Woods on the map.

If they only knew.

"Needless to say, I think I'll stick to watching from the sidelines from now on." He grinned, and catching Emily's eyes, gave her a wink.

Emily's face flushed. She turned to Max, refusing to meet Scott's eye again. "Well, Max, it looks like it's all you, then."

"What can I say? I think I'm as in love with Lucy's pies as I am with my own fiancée," Max joked. Then turning to Scott he explained, "It was actually right at this very counter that I first realized I was in love with Holly."

"Let me guess," Emily said, "you were eating a slice of pie while you were at it?"

Max lifted his hands helplessly. "I was smitten."

"You know, I probably made that pie," Emily said. "Lucy and I always share the task."

"Well, then I'll give a toast to you at our wedding," Max said gallantly. Elbowing Scott he said in a loud whisper, "Clearly, the woman knows her way to a man's heart."

That she does, Scott thought as his chest tightened. He shifted his gaze to Emily, whose face showed no sign of losing its pink glow anytime soon. He smiled to himself, looking down at his feet to spare her further attention. She hadn't outgrown it, in all these years. He used to love to tease her in school until she blushed, until he knew he'd gotten to her.

"Or at least the way to his stomach." Emily refilled Max's coffee and poured a fresh mug for him.

"Is Lucy at the bakery?" Scott asked, glancing around the crowded diner for his sister.

Emily's face took on a worried expression. "She felt like avoiding the hustle and bustle, and they were short-staffed here today."

Scott felt his brow furrow with concern, and he peered out the far window, hoping for a glimpse of his sister in the storefront across the road, wishing he could make things better. She was probably upset about their father, and why shouldn't she be? She didn't know who he was, not like Scott did.

Scott swallowed a swig of coffee. He was the last person to be comforting Lucy.

Lifting his chin, Max said, "Ready to talk about the project?"

"I'll let you two chat," Emily said, already backing away to take an order from a couple at the other side of the counter.

"I'll see you at the Spring Fling," Max said to her before her attention had fully faded. He turned to Scott and suggested, "You'll be there, too, right? We can all grab a drink or something."

Scott felt Emily's wide eyes lock with his. A shadow passed over her pale gray irises and a question sparked in her large pupils. Despite himself, he said, "That sounds great!"

Because it did. It sounded really, really great.

Emily watched from the corner of her eye as Scott and Max settled into a corner booth, a stack of rolled blueprints and paperwork spread between them. Her mind on anything but the job, she stopped herself just seconds before she overflowed Mr. Hawkins's coffee cup. His eyes narrowed with judgment when they met hers and she bit back an exasperated sigh. Mr. Hawkins was a regular at Lucy's Place. The diner wouldn't be the same without his familiar presence, but seriously, how much coffee could one old man consume?

"Can I get you anything to go with that, Mr. Hawkins?" She forced a pleasant smile and held his dark gaze patiently.

"Just another bowl of creamers," he grumbled.

Emily pinched her lips and nodded before sliding a fresh bowl of creamers to the side of his coffee mug. "Anything else?"

Mr. Hawkins held her gaze with challenge, and she straightened her spine. They both knew he didn't plan to order anything—he never did—but she couldn't help herself. Once or twice a week, she liked to encourage him to eat something, if not for Lucy and

George, then for himself. He was painfully thin and she knew that since his wife had died, all hope of a hot meal had probably disappeared with her. She smiled, relaxing her shoulders, and made a mental note to bring a pie over to him one day. He'd enjoy it. Even if he'd never admit it.

The sandwiches Max and Scott had ordered were up, and she slid them off the hot plate and balanced them on her palm and forearm, grabbing a fresh pot of coffee with her free hand. It still amazed her that she could do this—ten years ago when she started working at Lucy's Place she often came home in tears. Lucy and George had been patient with her, despite the chaos she caused. "Waitressing is underrated!" Lucy would quip with an encouraging smile, and sure enough, Emily had gotten the knack after awhile. Now and then, Lucy still broke out into random laughter when she recalled Emily sitting on the floor, broken plates surrounding her, covered in three customers' orders and a butter knife stuck in her hair.

The two men were deep in conversation, hunched over the table, and oblivious to her presence as she rounded the counter and strode to their table. "Here you go," she said cheerfully, her heart flip-flopping as she caught Scott's eye. He smiled and looked down quickly, causing her chest to swell with sudden hope.

Nervous. He said she made him nervous.

Scott cleared some papers away to make room for the plates, and she set them down, squaring her shoulders as she stood again. "Can I get you anything else?" she asked, eyeing their mugs. Max's mug was still full

and as she began to walk away, Scott tipped his own mug back, devouring the dregs.

"A refill would be great."

Well, that was interesting. She paused and tightened her grip on the handle of the coffeepot, planning her next move. It was ridiculous to think this way, truly masochistic. The man had shattered her heart and fled town. He was just being friendly. Or thirsty. There was nothing to read into. The facts were what they were and the fact was that Scott Collins wasn't going to be a regular in this place. No matter how badly she wished he would be. They were just two people who used to know each other. Two people who shared a moment in time. A moment that was long over.

"Are you going to be around the building later tonight?" he asked.

Her pulse stilled and she forced a breath before she replied evenly, "Probably…" She noted Max's amused grin from the corner of her eye and gritted her teeth. Must be easy for him to find this funny now that he was living in domestic bliss with Holly. How soon he had forgotten what it was like to be single. "Guess it depends on what time I get out of here tonight," she said briskly, forcing all her attention on Scott as she did her best to ignore the sparkle in Max's electric blue eyes.

Why? she wanted to ask. *Why does it matter if I will be home tonight? Why do you want to know?*

"Why?" she blurted, unable to stop herself.

Scott's expression froze. She waited, heart pounding, for his answer. "Just wondered," he said, breaking her stare, and Emily bit back a fresh wave of fury. Great, so she looks eager and he's just wondering!

"Well, enjoy your meal," she said and turned her back to refill Mr. Hawkins's coffee cup before he could start complaining.

Scott bit into his sandwich and chewed thoughtfully, trying his best to concentrate on the project details in front of him and not on the sight of Emily's slim hips as they swayed ever so alluringly away from the table. He rubbed his jaw, agitated. He was getting too used to her presence. And no good could come from that. For either of them.

"You know Emily well?"

Scott met Max's inquisitive gaze and shrugged. "We grew up together more or less. We went to school together. She was a year behind me."

"High school sweethearts?"

Scott narrowed his eyes but detected no menace in Max's expression. He was a decent guy. A guy's guy. Someone he'd probably be good friends with outside this town. They were roughly the same age, and both had a straightforward head for business. And a weakness for the women of Maple Woods, it would seem.

Scott shook his head. "Nothing serious," he lied.

Max nodded thoughtfully but something told Scott he wasn't buying it. Was it that obvious? He set down his sandwich and focused on the blueprints. Emily's presence was a distraction he couldn't afford right now, or ever. Max had commissioned Collins Construction to rebuild the library—a project that was budgeted for enough money for Scott to sit up and take seriously.

A real estate tycoon by profession, it was evident that Max knew the ins and outs of a project this size.

From the small bit of research Scott had done on Hamilton Properties, Max had more than ten years of experience with retail and commercial development projects of a much larger scale than the Maple Woods Library.

"So I have to ask," Scott said. "Why invest in the rebuilding of the library? It doesn't seem to fit with the rest of your portfolio."

"Interesting question." Max chewed his club sandwich and sprinkled his fries with salt from the shaker. "I guess you could say my priorities have changed since I moved to Maple Woods. I came here to build a shopping mall, and ended up deciding I couldn't ruin the integrity of the town."

Integrity. A bitter taste filled Scott's mouth and he coated it with a mouthful of fries when what he really wanted was a cooling slice of that lemon meringue that was perched on the counter over near Emily...Emily. He broke his stare, catching Max watching him, and took a swig of his coffee.

"I'm told you're aware of my sister's involvement in this," he said, lowering his tone. "My nephew is a good kid."

"I agree, and Lucy and George are like family," Max added. Lightening the mood, he grinned. "It's nice that we can partner up and make things right for this project."

"About that—"

Across from him, Max's brow pinched. "Something wrong?"

"I have my own construction business back in Seattle, and as you can imagine, they can't operate without me for the duration this project will take."

Max frowned. "What do you propose?"

"I'm sure you're aware that my father is in poor health." He gauged Max's simple nod by way of response. "He's not expected to recover."

"I heard. I'm sorry." Max didn't feign surprise or overt emotion and Scott felt his shoulders ease, grateful to be able to keep the conversation focused.

"Yes, well…" He cleared his throat and shuffled through the papers until he found a printout of the plan he had compiled that morning in preparation for this meeting. He handed it to Max, who studied it carefully. "I've decided to take Collins Construction on as a subsidiary of my own company. This will allow me to hire the appropriate crew and overseers for the project."

It would also allow him, he knew, to take responsibility for what had happened to Richard Porter—to own the mistakes his father had tried to bury, to repair what could be fixed, even though the broken life the Porters had lived at his hand could never be glued back together.

"So you'll essentially manage it from Seattle?"

"Yes."

Max rubbed his chin thoughtfully, finally tilting his head in acceptance. "As long as the job gets done, I can't argue. You know what you're doing, and I trust you to handle the project as you see fit. I guess my one question for you is this…Why the hell do you want to get out of this town so badly?

"That obvious, huh?"

Max rose his eyebrows in response at the same time that Emily reappeared at their table to refill their water.

There was one reason Scott was desperate to get out of town. It wasn't his father. It wasn't even the business. Or the memories. The reason was the person standing less than two feet away from him. The person that was strangely starting to look like every reason to stay, rather than to go.

Twelve years ago he knew he would rather never see Emily again than lie to the girl he loved. And twelve years later, it was still the truth. He loved her, damn it. No amount of time was going to change that, and no amount of wishing was going to undo the reason they could never be together.

Chapter Seven

The caw of the crows through the half-open window next to her bed woke Emily as the first crack of sunlight peeked over the treetops in the distance. She rolled over and glanced at the clock on her bedside table. Then, with a groan, she flipped back over, snuggling deeper under the duvet, squeezing her eyes shut. She wished she could stay in bed all day, but it wasn't possible. Even though Sweetie Pie didn't open for another four hours, she knew she had to go in early to get a jump start on the baking.

They'd kept her at the diner until closing last night, which had its perks, really. After Scott's strange mood yesterday, she wasn't sure what was running through that handsome mind. She could spend the rest of her life wondering why Scott had treated her as he had, she could force it out of him, or she could see it for what it had been. Two young kids. Ancient history. Who was she to punish him for the sins of his past?

All the same, having a valid reason to avoid coming home last night had put her at ease just as the thought of another confusing conversation made her gut tighten. She didn't need to be falling for him all over again, and the more time she spent with him, the more she increased the odds of that happening. When she'd counted her tips last night, she'd known the extra shift was worth the effort double-fold. Her plan was to pay the rent for this place for six months out, just to give Julia a cushion and ease the blow of her departure. If she even ended up getting accepted to that cooking school, that is. Yesterday's mail had once again brought nothing but a stack of bills and catalogs for clothes neither she nor her sister could afford.

A knock on the door caught her attention and she turned to see Julia standing in the open doorway, looking hesitant. "I thought I saw you moving around. I didn't wake you, did I?"

"No," Emily said, her voice tight. It was the first exchange the sisters had shared since their argument the other night. She thought she was over it, but now she realized Julia's words still stung a bit. "I was going to make blueberry pancakes," Julia offered, her expression hopeful enough to make Emily soften her stance. "You interested?"

Emily glanced at the clock. "Sure, so long as it's quick. I need to be at Sweetie Pie's soon to get a start on today's menu."

Relief swept Julia's face as she bounded away, and the sound of pans clanking in the kitchen quickly followed. With a long, tired sigh, Emily pushed back the blankets and sat up, rolling her feet onto the old oak floors. Outside her window, the sun had fully risen, and the rain from the past two days seemed to have dried. It would be nice if this weather held up for the Spring Fling, she thought, and then noticed the hope she still felt over the possibility of seeing Scott there.

She frowned as she tied her lightweight robe around her waist, remembering some of the sweet things he had said to her back in high school, in those magical days and nights when they were finally free of everyone's prying eyes. She grit her teeth, banishing the memories. She wasn't a teenager anymore. Those words didn't matter now.

"Thanks for making breakfast," Emily said as she wandered into the kitchen and poured herself a mug of coffee from the freshly brewed pot. "This is a nice surprise."

"Figured it was the least I could do for upsetting you." Julia whirled around and met her gaze, her green eyes murky with concern. "I feel really bad."

"Let's forget about it," Emily said as she stirred a teaspoon of sugar into her coffee. She tapped the spoon against the rim of her mug and set it down. "Besides, you made some good points."

She took in a breath, wondering if now was the time to come clean about applying to the culinary school in Boston. After the speech Julia had given her the other night, she was starting to think her concern that Julia would feel let down or betrayed was all in her own head. All this time Julia thought Emily was fine with things as they were—that she didn't long for more out of her own life—and nothing could have been further from the truth. Emily *did* want more. A lot more. The problem was that none of it was really in her control. The school could reject her just as easily as Scott had—the two things she wanted most. She couldn't have both. She might not even get one.

She stopped herself right there. What was she thinking? She and Scott were just exes now. There was nothing more to it than that.

Then why, she wondered, as she slid into her usual chair at the small kitchen table, did it feel like there might still be something between the two of them?

"I made some good points? Really?" Julia brightened as she turned back to the stove and plated the slightly burned pancakes. "Oops. The edges are a little black." Her face darkened with guilt and Emily bit the inside of her check. "Guess you should never turn your back on pancakes."

"They cook pretty quickly," Emily agreed and then shrugged, "Come on. I'm sure they're delicious. A little syrup will cover up any of the crunchy bits."

They sat in companionable silence, eating their breakfast and leafing through the catalogs that had gathered on the kitchen table. Several times Emily opened her mouth to tell Julia about the application she had sent in, but each time she thought she could mention it, her heart would pound so loudly she had to stop herself. Up until now, the application was her own special secret. If she didn't get in, it would be her own quiet loss. If she did…well, wouldn't that be the more appropriate time to share the news? When there was actually news to share at all?

"Spring Fling's tomorrow," Julia mused.

Emily's pulse skipped a beat. "That's right," she

said, forcing a casual tone. Feigning disinterest, she flicked a page in the catalog.

"I wonder if Scott's going," Julia continued.

Refusing to feed into her sister's overt insinuations, Emily took a large bite of the nearly inedible pancakes and leaned in closer to the catalog. It was useless. The page blurred and all she could see was Scott's face. That boyish grin that tugged one side of his mouth, the sheepish way he'd glance at the ground and back up at her. Her heart started to flutter.

"With everyone in town attending, I wasn't sure what his plans would include," Julia was saying. "But when I talked to him last night, he told me he was thinking about going."

Emily snapped her eyes to Julia's grinning face. Her mind whirled as her breath went still. Julia's bright green eyes sparked and she hid her growing smile behind the rim of her mug.

"You talked to Scott last night?" Emily clarified.

"Uh-huh." Julia smiled and casually cut into her pancakes. "Oh," she said, bringing her fingers to her lips. "These are delicious if I do say so myself."

"Julia." Emily stared at her sister, imagining a hundred different turns a conversation between her sister and Scott could have taken. "When did you talk to him?"

Julia regarded her quizzically. "I told you. Last night."

Growing impatient, Emily forced a deep breath. Her sister was having quite a bit of fun with this, but Emily didn't find it amusing in the least. In fact, she downright cared. Too much.

"Yes, but when last night? Did you run into him somewhere?"

"He stopped by here." Julia lifted an eyebrow. "He was looking for you."

Emily felt herself pale. So he had been serious when he'd asked her if she'd be around last night. But why?

"He wanted to return the pie plate," Julia continued, motioning to the cleaned and empty pie plate sitting on the counter.

Well, that about summed it up.

Emily shrank back in her seat, and stared listlessly at her plate of burned pancakes. She knew she had no right to feel as disappointed as she did, but nevertheless her heart felt heavy. She was getting hopeful, setting herself up for a fall, wishing for something that wasn't there, for someone who was long gone, just passing through. For someone who wasn't hers to miss anymore.

"He asked about you," Julia added, and Emily felt her pulse skip.

"Really?" She cut into her pancakes, attempting to cover her rising hope with the taste of charred batter.

"He seemed genuinely let down that you weren't here."

Emily sat back in her chair and gave her sister a level stare. "Maybe he was afraid you'd give him the third degree again."

Julia laughed and waved her hand through the air. "Oh, please. He knows my bark is worse than my bite. I always used to tease him when he'd come over."

Emily smiled at the memory. There seemed to be no greater amusement to the young Julia than spying on her sister and Scott, building up their romance to be so much more than it was in the end.

"So what happened then?" she dared to ask.

Julia shrugged. "I invited him in. He hesitated at first, but he couldn't think of an excuse quick enough for me, so I gave him a beer and we talked."

Emily dropped her chin and stared at her sister. "Beer? Since when do we have beer?"

"Since I bought some yesterday on my way home from work. You know, just in case we had any male suitors…"

Emily held up her hands. "Okay, then what happened?"

Julia took a sip of her coffee and pinched her lips. "My, my, aren't we suddenly curious? And here I thought you were no longer interested in the comings and goings of Scott Collins?"

"Are you going to tell me how the conversation went?" Emily's voice felt shrill, even to her own ears.

"Maybe you should ask him yourself," Julia said with a sly smile, and Emily let out a shaky sigh.

"Fine," she said briskly, pushing back her chair to stand. "I will."

Julia's smile widened. "I thought you'd say that."

Emily paused from picking up the dishes. "Thought or hoped?"

Julia seemed to consider this for a moment. "Both, I think. Yes, both." She shrugged. "Just in case you see him today, why don't you borrow my black cotton sundress?"

Emily hesitated. "Thanks. I will. But not because I want to impress him or anything," she added in a rush.

"Sure."

"I mean it, Julia. Scott and I are just exes. Now he's in town, and we're behaving like civil adults. There's nothing more to it than that."

"Is that what you really want?" Julia gave her a hard stare and crossed one long leg over the other.

Emily released a long sigh and set the dishes in the sink. She turned the tap on high. "It doesn't matter what I think. Scott has his own ideas."

"Oh, that he does," Julia said.

Emily whipped around to face her sister. "What's that supposed to mean?"

"Emily, I saw the way he looked at you the other night. He still cares about you."

Emily hesitated. "You're not making any sense," she muttered.

"I know I gave him a hard time the other night, but I wanted to see his reaction. I wanted to see if he felt bad for what he did to you all those years ago."

"And what did you deduce?" As much as Emily was trying to tell herself not to care, she couldn't help it. She had so many unanswered questions, and if Julia could give insight into the situation, then she wanted to hear it.

"He still cares about you, Emily. I thought maybe he'd be a jerk about it, brush it off, but he didn't," she said. "You saw for yourself. He looked like he felt genuinely...guilty."

Emily hesitated. "Maybe," she shrugged, turning back to the sink.

"So has he told you why he left like that, then?"

Emily tossed her hands up in the air, spraying soapy water onto the counter. "It doesn't matter now, Julia.

That was half a lifetime ago. It's over. He's moved on. It doesn't change anything."

"Sure it can," Julia said easily. "I see two people who might still have feelings for each other who aren't being honest about where things broke down." Julia set a hand on Emily's arm. "You'll always wonder, Emily. You might have been too hurt back then to ask, but now is your chance to find out. Once you know, then you can move forward."

Emily tried to ignore the implication that she hadn't gotten over Scott yet. She let out an exasperated sigh. "I told you! He's not even staying for long. He might not even be back."

Julia just shrugged. "All the more reason to ask then. It's now or never."

"Why are you pushing this, Julia?"

"I just see two people who meant a lot to each other who have a lot of things left to say," Julia said. "I say it like I see it, Em. What can I say? I'm a hopeless romantic."

Emily blinked, wondering if she should take her sister's opinion to heart or not. Julia had a way of getting ahead of herself, letting imagination take control, but she wouldn't be so careless when it came to Emily's well-being. If Julia thought that Scott still cared about her, then maybe her sister was onto something.

But no… Emily frowned, thinking of the things Lucy had told her yesterday, the way Scott was so eager to get out of their parents' house. Out of town. His bags were still packed and waiting. He'd rented a car.

Disappointment tugged at her again. Scott had cared for her once, and maybe a part of him still had some lingering fondness for the time they'd shared. But there was no room for her in his life. There hadn't been for the past twelve years and there wouldn't be for the next.

Hopeless romantic. Emily shook her head. That's exactly what Julia was. But when it came to herself and Scott only one word in that phrase applied: *hopeless*.

Scott leaned back against the old bench swing on his sister's front porch and gazed over the hedge onto Main Street, for once looking to the center of town and all its buzz as an escape. Anything felt more desirable than sitting here, having a heart-to-heart with his sister.

Lucy pushed open the screen door and handed him a glass of iced coffee, taking a long sip from her own as she joined him on the swing. It creaked under the weight of their two bodies and began to sway slowly, naturally. They sat there quietly, as though no time had lapsed and they had never been apart. Scott glanced up at the back of the diner at the corner of the narrow side street the Miller cottage was nestled on.

He studied the second story of the building, trying to remember the exact layout of Lucy's old apartment—well, Emily's apartment now. If the bedrooms were across from the living room then, yep, the windows all the way to the left corner were the bedroom windows.

Realizing he was staring like some Peeping Tom into the bedroom windows of the Porter sisters, he jerked away his gaze, his pulse kicking up a notch as the fire escape door flew open and Emily appeared on the metal landing.

Beside him, Lucy chuckled and called out, "Emily?" Under her breath she muttered, "What is that girl up to?"

Having reached the ground, Emily swiveled toward the house, alarm transforming her features when she registered her audience. "Oh. Hi." Her normally pleasant smile was replaced with something tight and stilted.

Scott raised a hand by way of hello, matching his sister's effort.

"You off to the bakery?" Lucy inquired.

Emily hesitated. Frowning, she looked around helplessly, as if searching for someone else to come along and answer the question for her. Scott watched her heave a sigh and then take a few long strides toward the cottage.

"I was going to get an early start on the baking," she explained as she reached the bottom of the porch steps. She glanced at him and then quickly away.

"That a new dress?" Lucy asked.

Emily glanced down at herself and gave a modest shrug. "I borrowed it from my sister." She cast another brief look in his direction and then looked down at her black cotton sundress.

"I think it's cute," Scott said before he could stop himself. The heat from his sister's sidelong glance was enough to melt the ice in his glass, and he felt a rush of warmth creep its way up his neck.

After a deliberate pause that Scott would later pay her back for, Lucy said, "I agree, Em."

"Oh, well…" Her eyes darted to his and she quickly

looked down and dragged her foot through a patch of dirt.

The silence felt like an eternity and when Scott turned from Emily's reddening cheeks to focus on the ice cubes in his glass, he could almost hear them crackling.

"Well, I should go," Emily said at last, and Scott felt a twinge of disappointment.

His gaze lingered on her as she walked back toward the diner, her shoulders squared and proud, before she strangely seemed to break into a sprint as soon as she rounded the corner.

"I wonder what that girl is up to," Lucy mused. "She seemed to be almost running from something, taking the back stairs and all."

Scott had the unsettling suspicion that she had been running from him. Not that he could fault her.

"If I didn't know better, I'd say Emily seemed a little flustered around you." Lucy took a slow sip of her drink, staring casually ahead into the distance. "If I didn't know better, that is."

"Please. Emily and I are ancient history."

"If you say so," Lucy said archly.

Scott snorted. He couldn't deny the disappointment—or relief—he'd felt last night when he'd finally just marched over to the door down the hall and knocked on it, ready to come clean, ready to set things right, only to learn that Emily wasn't even home. The thought of hurting her again killed him—but the thought of leaving this town without telling her everything was worse.

She deserved the truth.

"I say so," he said, but his heart said something altogether different. "We were just kids when we dated. That rarely amounts to anything."

"George and I were just kids when we got married, and look at us now," Lucy pointed out.

Scott bristled. "That's…different."

"Maybe so. And I can't say it's always been easy. Financially, that is."

Scott dragged a hand down his face. He didn't like to think of his sister worrying about money when he had so much. But she was a proud woman, a hardworking woman. An honest woman. "Sometimes I think about how different life would have been if I'd stayed," he said, catching himself only after he'd spoken.

Beside him, he heard his sister sigh. "Oh, well. Maybe it's for the best, really. Look at how far you've come."

He turned to her, his temper stirring when he thought of his father and the lingering consequences of the choice he had made all those years ago. He took a long sip of his iced coffee, waiting for it to cool him, slow his racing pulse.

"Mom and Dad never wanted me to stick around. They told me if I married Emily, I could forget being a part of the family business. They ever tell you that?" He glanced at his sister sidelong, noting the dismay in her expression, and the lack of surprise.

"They never agreed with the choice I made to marry young, and you know that. They wanted something else for you. Something more. You'd been accepted to a great college. They didn't want you to squander opportunities. They thought they were doing what was best for you."

She really didn't get it. It was better that way, he

told himself firmly, before he steered the conversation in a direction it never needed to go. "Well, funny that now I'm suddenly needed so badly at the family company," he said bitterly.

"You're older now, Scott. It's different." She paused. "So there's really nothing left between you and Emily?"

Scott stared into his glass. "Nope."

"You two do look good together," Lucy mused.

"Lucy." His tone was firm. She couldn't drag him down this path. He wouldn't let her. He had to be strong and fight these feelings. "Stop. You know I'm not in town for long."

"I know." She sighed. "I was just hoping you would change your mind. I guess I thought maybe you might find a reason to stay."

"And you thought that reason might be Emily?" How little she knew. A moment of weakness caused him to wonder if he should set her straight. But he couldn't, not yet. First he needed to tell Emily, and find a way to set things right as best he could. He needed to take responsibility for his actions.

And he needed to see if somehow, someway, he could make her believe in him again.

Emily sighed as she hung her apron on the hook and smoothed the black dress Julia had lent her. Another long, busy day at the bakery had kept her distracted, but now, as the last customer settled their bill, all those uncertainties came swimming back to the forefront. She couldn't shake the image of Scott sitting on Lucy's porch this morning—she'd purposefully gone out of her way to avoid him by taking the back stairs, but the spark of excitement she felt when she saw him was undeniable.

It was the fatigue talking, she told herself. There was so much going on all at once with Scott being back, the bakery opening, and of course, the possibility that she might be accepted to culinary school. All at once life had gone from being painfully routine to bewilderingly unpredictable.

The first week at the bakery had been a success, but not without a lot of hard work and effort. Emily glanced at Lucy, who was looking over the books, tallying up the profits, and felt a twinge of dread. She'd applied to that school in Boston back when she was working at the diner, pouring coffee and shuffling orders to and from the kitchen. Now she felt queasy when she thought of the opportunity she was giving up—of how much she was needed here, and how much Lucy depended on her.

"We had a good week, Em," Lucy said, still focused on the spreadsheets in front of her. "Why don't you get out of here early? I'll finish off the rest of the pies for tomorrow's festival."

Emily frowned. "You sure?" The Spring Fling was already tomorrow, and they still had two dozen mini-pies to bake for the pie-eating contest.

"Go home," Lucy said. "That's an order from your boss."

Emily smiled tiredly. "Thanks, Lucy. See you tomorrow, then?"

"Sure, we can all go together," Lucy suggested, looking up from her paperwork. "Scott's coming, too."

Emily paused. "That sounds like fun," she managed. Too much fun. If she knew what was good for her, she would stay away from Scott and focus on the future, not the past.

With a wave, she pushed out into the late afternoon sunshine, walking quickly in an effort to pound out any fleeting hopes that had no place in her current life. She halted when she saw Scott walking casually down the street, and then slowly resumed her path.

No place at all, she reminded herself. Scott had taken those hopes with her when he left town, and he'd take them with him again if she let him.

Emily turned her key in the side door that led to the staircase and the rooms above the diner, but it was no use. Scott was coming closer now, he'd seen her, and when she dared to steal a look in his direction, he held up a hand. Her pulse skipped a beat as his bright blue eyes shone in the sunlight.

"How was work today?" he asked, coming to stand next to her. As his eyes roamed over her face, she held her breath, thinking of what Julia had suggested that morning.

"Busy," she said. "But I suppose that's a good thing." She fumbled with her key, but her hands were beginning to tremble.

"You've been putting in long hours," he commented. "I stopped by to see you last night, but your sister said you were still working."

See her? So it hadn't just been to return the pie plate.

"Yes, Julia mentioned that." She bit her lip. "I… hope she didn't give you a hard time."

Scott smiled affably. "Nah. We had a nice conversation, actually."

"Oh?" Emily's mind began to whirl with possibilities.

"Yeah, we reminisced a bit. She caught me up on some of the happenings around town." He shrugged. "She really looks up to you."

Emily frowned. "Oh?".

Scott's grin widened. "She couldn't sing your praises enough."

Oh, Julia. Emily felt her cheeks flush and she forced the key abruptly, fearing for a moment she had snapped it in half, and then let herself into the darkened vestibule. A stack of letters sat at her feet, having fallen out of the open mailbox. She bent down to retrieve the pile, aware of Scott's presence behind her as she did so. Straightening her spine, she kept her back to him for the length of a good hard breath before she whirled again to face him. Her heart dropped with longing as her gaze met his handsome features.

Damn it, was there ever going to be a day where the sight of that chiseled jaw and those twinkling eyes didn't leave her physically aching? His presence was so all-consuming, that when she was alone with him like this, she forgot to breathe. Attraction this deep was dangerous. And rare. No wonder she had never been able to shake the image of him. No wonder, despite how deeply he had hurt her, she still dared to dream of him.

"You coming in?" Her voice was choked and breathless.

He held up a stack of blueprints and a binder nearly four inches thick with papers. "I'm heading over to the office, actually. It's easier when most of the people there have already left for the day."

Emily nodded. She understood how it felt to live in a town where you were the object of speculation and gossip.

"How are the plans for the library coming along?" She had been wondering how his meeting with Max had gone at the diner the day before. From what she could tell, the men hit it off well. She wasn't surprised though. The two had a lot in common. They were both successful, they were both charming and they both seemed to hold a sadness in their eyes at times despite their heart-melting grins.

"I think we'll start construction in about six weeks," Scott said, revealing nothing as Emily locked his gaze, searching for more insight. She couldn't deny the flutter of hope that filled her chest: Did he plan to stay until then? A lot could happen in six weeks.

She waited for him to elaborate, but when he did not, she volunteered, "I'm sure the town will be thrilled. It was the children's wing that was damaged, right?" She motioned to the blueprints, curiosity getting the better of her. "Can I see?"

Scott raised his eyebrows in surprise but he looked pleased as he set down his binder and unraveled the blueprints, awkwardly spreading them against the inside of the door as he crossed into the vestibule. As he spread the blueprints out wide, she oohed and ahhed over the truly beautiful design, but her gaze lingered firmly on Scott's biceps, which flexed as he adjusted the large scroll. His golf shirt stretched under the width of his broad shoulders. She traced the contours of his back with her eyes, imaging her fingers skimming all the way down to his waist. And beyond.

"I can't take credit for the design," Scott said,

shrugging as he began rolling the print. "My dad brainstormed that part with an architect."

"Well, he did a great job. He should be proud."

Scott's smile fell. Instantly, Emily regretted saying anything, but Scott had opened the door to the conversation. What was it between Scott and his father? It went beyond him not wanting to discuss his father's declining health. Noticing the way Scott's jaw twitched and his mouth took the form of a thin, grim line, Emily pondered what could keep someone this angry at their own parent for this long. Especially under the current circumstances.

"I hope Lucy likes it," Scott said and then quickly added, "I know she was really upset about Bobby's part in it."

Emily smiled kindly. "It was an accident. At least no one was hurt."

Scott nodded and seemed to swallow hard, taking pause at her words. Emily glanced down at the mail in her hands, realizing she had overstepped, and her breath caught when she noticed the return address on the top envelope. The culinary school in Boston.

"I should probably get to the office," Scott said, and Emily couldn't help but detect a thread of disappointment in his tone.

She nodded, unable to bring herself to speak. She clenched the envelopes in her hands until she felt them become slick with the sweat from her palms, but Scott made no movement toward the door.

"What did you want to talk about?" Emily asked suddenly, pulling herself from the thoughts whirling through her head as she stared at the letter. "Last night, when you stopped by."

Scott's gaze pierced through hers, until her heart started to race from more than the possibility of her fate tucked inside the sealed envelope.

After a beat he said, "Nothing that can't wait."

Emily frowned. "I have time."

"I wanted to thank you for the pie again." He grinned.

The pie plate. Emily internally scowled. Julia had obviously built the visit up to be more than it was. Much more.

Scott held up his blueprints, flashing her a grin. "I should really get going."

Emily tried to hide her disappointment.

"See you later, then."

She watched him take the three steps down to the sidewalk, lifting her hand as he turned back to wave his blueprints at her, and then she leaned back against the wall, closing her eyes, listening to the pounding of her heart.

Glancing down at the letter in her hands she held it up to the light, pursing her lips when she was unable to make out any of the words written inside. Her entire future was in this envelope, all her hopes for something more in life.

Without stopping to think about what she was doing, she ripped open the envelope as quickly as she could, not bothering to care about the rough jagged edge she had forced with her fingertip. She pulled the letter from the sleeve, her chest heaving with emotion, her hands shaking as her eyes skimmed the page so quickly, she only made out random phrases rather than the collective point.

By the time she reached the bottom she burst out

laughing. A change in the fall schedule. They had sent her a letter about a modification in the course catalogue! Depleted of energy, she sat down on the bottom step and waited for her breathing to return to normal as she folded the letter back into the badly torn envelope and tucked it into her handbag.

She was spared the demand of being forced into a decision. Only a matter of months ago when she had sent in her application, she had thought this was all she wanted. The chance to hone her skills, pursue her passion. The chance to start over and be herself and define herself by her future, not her past. Suddenly, she wasn't sure that was even what she wanted.

The only man she had ever loved was back in town. For how long, she didn't know. A part of her wanted to run from him, run from the town that had caused her such pain, that reminded her of her loss everywhere she turned. It was exactly what her sister had accused her of doing—avoiding more heartache.

A few months ago she had thought sending in her application was taking a risk. That starting life over in a new town with new people was the biggest leap of faith she could ever make, that it would take courage she didn't even know she had. But now…now she wondered if sticking around and dealing with the life she had been given was the biggest risk of all.

Chapter Eight

Scott glanced down at the date on his email and blinked. Nearly a week had passed since he'd first driven into town, and against his reservations, he was beginning to think he might miss the place when he was gone. His gut twisted when he thought of the day when he would get in his rental car and drive away, this time knowing he would never be welcome to return.

Closure, they said, did wonderful things for the healing process. Well, he was banking on it. In Seattle he lived an anonymous life, free of the burden of his past. His friends there knew nothing of him other than what he chose to reveal. The brief relationships he'd had over the years never amounted to more than casual flings—the common complaint among the women he'd dated was that he had too many walls up, that they never felt they knew the real him. Scott had let them go, knowing they were right, hoping that eventually he would meet someone he could trust enough to be himself with, trust enough to take down the mask and expose the man beneath.

He just never expected that person would be Emily. After all these years, she was still the only one who could reach him.

Scott ran his hand over the stubble on his jaw and released a long sigh as he tore his thoughts from Emily and tried to focus on the chain of emails that had collected in his in-box over the past few days. Two major projects were scheduled to break ground next month, and he probably had another week—two at best—before they'd need him back in the office. He supposed in a pinch he could fly in for a few days and then come back, but that was dangerous thinking. The sooner he severed himself from Maple Woods, and everyone in it, the better. The longer he was in town, the easier it was to think of what might have been. He clicked on the next email, pushing away the thought that refused to budge.

His stomach began to burn and he peeled another antacid free of its wrapper and set the roll back on the table. From the window in his room above the diner, his eyes rested on the festivities below, where a large tent was being set up in the middle of the town square. It was one of the few days of the year that Lucy's Place closed down, and Scott could sense how much Lucy was looking forward to eating food she hadn't cooked. He chewed on the chalky coating in his mouth. Chances were high that Emily felt the same way.

Scott leaned forward in his chair and forced his eyes to the computer screen, where he worked without stopping for the next few hours. After a quick shower and shave, he stepped out into the hall, careful to keep an ear out for Emily, but the building was silent. He pushed through the back door and jogged down the fire escape. Lucy and George were already on their porch when he strolled past the overgrown hydrangea bushes blooming with blue, purple and pink flowers.

"Bobby's coming along later. With friends," Lucy informed him after he'd greeted his brother-in-law, standing to smooth the skirt of her sundress.

"Shall we, then?" Scott gestured down the quiet street toward the center of town.

"Not yet," Lucy interrupted. "I asked Emily to join us."

Scott's eyebrows shot up as he met and locked his sister's eyes. He clenched and unclenched his fists as he waited for his temper to subside. "I thought you weren't going to play matchmaker anymore."

Lucy laughed easily and waved her hand through the air. "Settle down, Scott. I've given up any hopes of that. You're safe."

"Then—"

Lucy narrowed her gaze. "This has nothing to do with you, Scott," she said sharply. "Emily is my co-worker and a very good friend of mine."

"I'm sorry," he huffed in response. He stared down the road, wondering what Emily thought about all this. It hadn't slipped his mind that Max Hamilton had suggested they all meet up for a drink at the event and that Emily had looked like a deer in the headlights.

"What ever happened between you and Emily?"

Scott whirled to face Lucy, his chest pounding. "What do you mean?" he asked, but the hardened edge in his tone only confirmed his guilt.

"You used to like her when you were kids and now..." Her eyes searched him, crinkling in confusion, her mouth a thin line of displeasure. She shook her head. "It's too bad. She's a really nice girl."

"I know that," Scott bit back.

"Then why do you get so shifty every time her name is mentioned? If you're worried about sending her the wrong message, I can assure you, you don't need to worry."

"What's that supposed to mean?"

Lucy tipped her head, a sadness taking over her features. "Emily keeps to herself. She doesn't date much, and she's the last person I know who would assume someone was interested in her romantically. Especially you."

"Why would you say that?"

Lucy gave him a knowing look. "You broke her heart." Scott began to protest but Lucy raised her hand to stop him. "You were eighteen then. It's forgivable. But you're a grown man, Scott. What's your excuse now?"

Scott stood at the base of the porch, his eyes shifting from Lucy to George and back again. *What's your excuse now?* He squared his jaw and thrust a fist into his pocket, his mind whirling somewhere between rage and hurt so deep he thought he might just shout out loud—scream out the truth of his actions, of his reasons behind breaking up with Emily. It was an excuse all right, and a damned good one. It would be sure to get his sister off his back about his interactions with Emily. But it might also kick her out of his life for good.

Suddenly brightening, Lucy waved over Scott's shoulder and shoved past him without another word, calling, "There you are!"

Scott turned to follow Lucy's gaze, his chest tightening as he saw Emily strolling up the sidewalk in a navy blue sundress and lavender cardigan, her chestnut hair flowing softly around her shoulders. Her smile was bright and unsuspecting, and Scott felt the knot in his stomach loosen, offering a smile in return as she met his gaze.

"Hi," he said, and then cleared his throat as his voice caught.

"Hey." Her voice was pleasant and sweet, the simple word so melodic that he longed for her to say something more.

"Ready to go?" Lucy asked, ignoring Scott altogether.

Emily stopped walking as they bridged the gap, and Scott soon found himself at her side, grateful for her nervous chatter that overshadowed the heavy, heated silence emanating from Lucy. When they arrived at the town square, Lucy muttered a quiet excuse and walked away with George in tow.

Scott turned to face Emily head on, finding her gray eyes bright, her full pink lips curving at the corners. "Alone again," he said with a slow smile he couldn't fight.

"That's becoming a theme with us." She held his gaze, perhaps in challenge, perhaps in curiosity.

Scott felt his pulse take speed. "Is that a good thing or not?" *Tell me, Emily, because I don't know anymore.*

His world seemed so clear when he was away from her, so black-and-white, so factual. He was responsible for her father's death. His father had covered the entire thing up. He would have to tell her. She would hate him. How could she not?

But when he was with her like this... Scott inhaled deeply. Everything was different when he was alone with Emily. The situation was as gray as the irises of her large searching eyes. All reason and strength left him, and all he wanted to do was grab her by the shoulders and press her close, to feel the smooth curves of her body against his, to beg her for forgiveness or maybe to never tell her at all, but instead to just go on like this...forever.

"Well," Emily said shyly. She lowered her eyes, causing Scott's gut to pull taught. Looking up, she said softly, "I was sort of thinking it was a good thing."

"I was hoping you would say that," he murmured, the release of the words sending a rush of air to his chest. Just admitting that one small truth lessened the burden that had weighed on him for so many years.

It was just like that age-old saying—*the truth shall set you free.* In this case, however, he couldn't help but wonder once again if the truth would do more harm than good.

Emily forced herself to remain as outwardly calm as possible, even though her heart was racing. Scott sat next to her on the grass under the shade of a large maple, resting his elbows on his knees. Sitting close to him like this, sipping at her ice-cold lemonade, Emily couldn't help but feel a twinge of sadness. It was just so perfect. So achingly, terrifyingly perfect.

She slid a glance at Scott, letting her eyes roam greedily over the broad width of his back, the wide, chiseled shoulders and the confident grace of his profile as he looked out onto the square, taking in the scene. She wondered what he was thinking, if being here made him want to stay. She sighed, fearing that it might make him just want to leave all the more.

Emily quickly looked around the square, hoping to spot a few friendly faces in the crowd. She spotted an older couple she recognized as regular guests of Holly's at The White Barn Inn and waved. With a sharp turn, the woman—Evelyn Adler—peered at her, her expression transforming into something altogether more interested when she noticed Scott.

"Well, hello there, young lady," Evelyn said to Emily as she approached, but her eyes rested firmly on Scott. The woman pinched her lips like a little bird while her deep blue eyes glimmered with awareness. "And *hello,*" she cooed to Scott, widening her gaze hopefully while her husband stood dutifully at her side. She patted her graying hair girlishly.

"Hello," Scott said pleasantly, though Emily detected an undertone of curiosity.

"I don't think we've had the pleasure of meeting," Evelyn purred, the intensity of her gaze sharpening like a hawk about to swoop in on its prey.

"I don't think so, either," Scott said, standing to extend his hand. At the gesture, Evelyn stepped back in shock, unabashedly raking her eyes over the length of his body as her lips curled into a hundred-watt smile. "Scott Collins. I just came back to town, so you must have moved here while I was away."

Emily was standing by now, brushing a bit of grass

and dirt off the skirt of her dress, and she noticed Max and Holly watching the exchange in the distance. Holly was shaking her head in dismay while Max laughed heartily. She waved them over as Evelyn continued, "Oh, we don't live here. We just visit every few months. Have you been to The White Barn Inn? It's *bliss*ful!"

"Well, thank you for the compliment!" Holly said as she joined the group. She slipped a wink to Emily and Emily nudged Max in the ribs. Scott's gaze passed over the three of them, clearly realizing that he was at a disadvantage when it came to the persistent Evelyn Adler.

"It's good to see you here, Emily," Evelyn said pointedly, making an obvious show of shifting her eyes to Scott and leaving them there. "It seems that Maple Woods is just bursting with lovebirds this year!"

Emily felt her face blanch. She could feel the steady shaking of Max's laughing torso beside her and she watched as Holly gave him a warning glance, fire in her eyes.

"We're old friends, Mrs. Adler," Emily said as her cheeks began to burn.

"Pity," Evelyn huffed, folding her arms across her fragile chest. She glared at Emily, as if this were somehow her fault. "A handsome man like this? In my day, men and women weren't just friends. But then, in my day, a woman didn't strut around town in pants, either." She clucked her tongue as her gaze lingered on Scott, and Emily could hear Max chuckling.

"Come on, Mrs. Adler," Holly said, taking the older woman by the elbow and giving Emily a knowing glance. "I've entered my raspberry preserves in a contest and the judging is about to start."

"Exciting times," Max said with mock enthusiasm, and Holly swatted him playfully. Undeterred, he shot a grin at Scott and said, "You gotta admit, this town's got a hell of a lot more going for it than we city guys are used to."

"Young man!" Evelyn's sharp cry punctured the din of nearby conversations. "Did you just *curse?*"

Affronted, Max took a step back and then pressed his lips together, laughter shining in his eyes. "Guilty as charged, Evelyn," he admitted, holding up two palms as he pleaded his innocence.

"Well…" Evelyn bristled, her brightly painted lips twisting coyly. "I could never stay mad at a young man as handsome as you."

With a chuckle, Max led the group away and Emily laughed to herself as Holly turned back and shook her head. "Sorry about that," she said to Scott, whose eyes were searching hers for some sort of explanation. "I didn't mean to throw you to the wolves."

"Who *is* that woman?"

"Evelyn Adler." Emily sighed, falling naturally into step beside him as they weaved their way through the stalls selling everything from local artwork to children's clothes. Julia was even selling a bunch of knitted goods she'd created on her downtime at the shop. "She's a regular at The White Barn Inn. She's a little eccentric, but we love her dearly."

They settled into a spot near the gazebo. Scott grew silent and rested his forearms on his knees. "So, old friends, huh?" He glanced at her sidelong, and Emily felt her stomach drop.

Her gaze fell to the grass, and she plucked a few dandelions before tossing them to the side. "Seemed like the easiest thing to say." She stole a glance in his direction, her breath catching at the intensity in his eyes.

"You were a hell of a lot more than just a friend to me," he said, and Emily looked away, frowning.

What was done was done. When her father died, she had learned to savor the moment, to not take the present for granted. Sometimes it was easy to lose sight of that, especially more recently when she was too busy getting lost in the future and all of its conflicting possibilities.

She straightened her shoulders. There would be no thinking about the future today. Today was all anyone really had.

A little shiver down her spine told her that today she had everything she had ever wanted, anyway.

"Tell me they won't do the Chicken Dance," Scott said with a grin as he watched the couples spin on the dance floor.

"Maybe the Hokey Pokey," Emily replied with a wink that sent a surge of heat straight to his groin. He tempered his desire with a sip of his beer. The sun had faded nearly an hour ago, and the band had picked up on its cue. Evelyn Adler was front and center on the dance floor, dragging her poor husband along for the ride. Max Hamilton lifted his hand in a wave and then twirled Holly until she threw her head back, laughing. Emily rubbed her arms as a cool breeze cut through the trees, rustling the leaves. It was all the ammunition he needed.

"Want to dance?" Scott asked with a slow smile, tipping his head in the direction of the dance floor, where half of the townspeople were bouncing around the band's whims.

Emily hesitated just long enough for him to wonder if he had stirred up an old wound and then turned to him with a smile that took his breath away.

"I'd love to," she said, hopping out of her folding chair. With one hand on the small of her back he guided her onto the makeshift dance floor and then curled his arm around her waist, his free hand taking hold of hers as they fell in step with the beat.

She kept her gaze lowered aside from a few telling glances from the hood of her lashes, her lips curling into a smile that pulled his heart so tight, he thought the ache would cut off his air. The music was too loud to make conversation possible, but Scott didn't mind. Without words, he could focus on her presence, on the way her smooth, soft palm felt so small in his own, and the way his arm rested so perfectly on the curve of her hip. He grazed the soft cotton of her dress with his fingertips, remembering how her bare body felt in his arms.

As the dance continued, he gradually pulled her closer, and she didn't resist, instead curling herself naturally into his chest, her chin hovering above his shoulder. He craned his neck and closed his eyes, drinking in the smell of her hair, feeling the pounding of her heart through his chest, wondering what it would be like to hold her like this forever.

If he tried hard enough he could almost be that kid again. The kid who had no awareness of what he had once done. The kid who was just crazy in love with Emily Porter.

Emily pulled back as the song ended, but he kept a hand on her hip, unable to let her go just yet. The strings of light cast a glow on her face, catching the glint in her eyes. Something deep within him began to stir.

"Want to take a walk?" he suggested, noticing that the band members were stepping aside from their instruments for a water break.

Emily nodded and they walked into the shadows of the trees, the buzz of the party behind them soon fading. The night was clear and quiet once they were well beyond the square, and the sound of crickets could be heard at random.

"I love that sound," Scott murmured.

"What sound?"

He stopped and leaned back against a fence post. "The sound of town, I guess. It's soothing."

Emily glanced around with a shrug. "I guess I don't even notice anymore."

"It's funny, you know? I've been gone for so long, I didn't think I would remember any of this, but being here…it's like no time has passed at all."

"I was thinking the same thing," Emily said with a small smile.

"I'm really sorry about how things left off with us, Emily," he said, his voice husky. *Just say it, just say it.* "I never meant to hurt you. Believe me when I say that I only ever wanted you to be happy. I still do."

Emily held his gaze, searching his eyes with hers as if trying to confirm the validity of his words. Eventually, she nodded. "I am happy," she said, and Scott felt a jolt. He hadn't seen that coming.

"Really?" he asked. He had to know.

"Everyone has sad times, Scott. You know that. But that doesn't mean I haven't been happy. I mean, look around…I get paid to do what I love. I have a great boss. I live with my sister, and even though she can be a handful, she's still my best friend. There are a lot of reasons to be happy."

"And now?"

"Am I happy right now? In this moment?" A smile played at her mouth. "I'm very happy."

He had taken so much from her, stolen her innocence with the blink of his eye. Yet here she was, standing before him with eyes soft and longing, lips parted and waiting. He could reach out and touch her; he could try to fill the part of her heart he had left empty. Her father was gone, and nothing could bring him back, but there was another wrong that Scott could set right. He had a chance, right now, here in this moment, to take back that day all those years ago and make her see how badly he had wanted her then. How much he still did.

He took a step forward, watching as Emily's eyes widened ever so slightly as he lowered his mouth to hers. His lips grazed hers softly, a caress so light it sent a shiver down the length of his spine, until her mouth parted to his, hesitantly at first as their tongues began their dance. He tightened his hold on her waist, pulling her body close to his chest until heat flared deep within him. Her hips pushed against his groin until his need grew with each lace of their tongues, and he claimed her mouth with determined energy, needing to be as close to her as she would allow him.

She sighed into his mouth as his kisses became urgent, but instead of pulling back as he feared, she dug her hands deep into his biceps and then up and around his shoulders, raking her fingers through his hair as their mouths persisted hungrily and their bodies fused. He could feel the swell of her breasts against his chest, and as desire drove him forward, he traced a hand around the curve of her hip, snaking his way up her stomach until he cupped her breast in his palm, feeling her chest rise and fall under his hand as her breathing became ragged.

Breaking the kiss, he locked eyes with her for the briefest of seconds before clutching her so close he felt he could break her, and she sighed into his ear as her hair cascaded down her back, glistening in the moonlight. He ran a hand through her chestnut locks, a memory seizing his chest as he rested his head on hers.

If they could just stay like this. If it could only be so easy.

Chapter Nine

"Well, there you are," Julia said as Emily shuffled into the kitchen, yawning. Leaning a hip against the butcher block, she added, "I was beginning to wonder if you made it home last night."

Emily glanced sleepily at the freshly brewed coffee and smiled. "Sorry I lost track of you at the festival," she said, filling her favorite mug. "Did you manage to sell a lot of your knitting samples?"

"Oh, the stand did fine enough, but when I couldn't find you anywhere, I got a little worried."

"Sorry, I should have called you." Emily sat down at the table and wrapped her fingers around her mug. She eyed the clock, making sure she didn't lose track of time.

Julia finished spreading some of Holly's raspberry preserves on her toast with quick, determined strokes.

She pursed her lips into a coy smile. "So I take it you and Scott had a nice time—"

"Oh, don't you start!" Emily cried, rolling her eyes. Across from her, Julia looked mesmerized, but for once she held her tongue. "Before you say anything, you should know that there's nothing going on between Scott and me. We've decided that we're just... old friends."

Just old friends who had kissed.

Julia held her gaze, her expression impassive, her head tipped. Finally she shrugged and bit into the corner of a triangle of toast. "If you say so."

Emily narrowed her eyes in suspicion. It wasn't like her sister to let things drop so easily. "Well, I do say so," she said with a huff. She blew at the steam curling up from her mug and took a tentative sip, her pulse twitching at the memory of last night.

She set the mug on the table. It was different now, she reassured herself. Scott was a grown man. He wasn't going to behave like a teenager and leave her hanging without so much as an acknowledgment.

"Well, I guess if you're just friends then you won't care that he stopped by here again, looking for you this morning," Julia said mildly.

"What? When?"

With a glimmer in her eyes, Julia pushed aside her plate of toast and met Emily halfway over the table. "About half an hour ago. I told him you were sleeping."

"What did he say?"

"He said he'd look for you later."

"He told you that?" Emily gasped.

Julia looked insulted. "Would I ever lie to you,

Em?" She sat back in her chair and played with the handle of her coffee mug.

"No, of course you wouldn't lie to me." Emily glanced at the clock once more. Realizing it was nearly time to leave for work, she gulped the rest of her coffee, hoping the heavy dose of caffeine might help clear all the conflicting emotions muddling her head.

She washed her mug in the sink and then turned to face Julia, who had already recovered and was grinning suggestively. With a knowing chuckle, Emily shook her head and patted her sister on the shoulder as she walked out into the hall, craning for the slightest sound behind Scott's door. With only a twinge of disappointment, she deduced he had left for the day, probably hard at work already. Last night he'd told her the library project was moving ahead and a crew was already on-site to clear out the rubble. What that meant for the two of them, she didn't know—she hissed in a breath, catching herself. *The two of them.* Was it really possible?

Emily pressed her lips together and hurried to the stairs, dropping her to hand to the rail as she quickened her step. She stopped at the landing when she spotted Scott standing in the vestibule at the base. The faintest furrow gathered between his brows when he looked up at her.

She paused at his hesitation and then offered a tentative smile. "Hi," she said.

"Hey," he said, shoving his hands into his pockets as she slowly took the remaining stairs. His low voice sent a shiver down her spine. She waited to see if he would reach out to her, touch her, give her a sign that last night hadn't been a fleeting occasion. A mistake.

But all he did was stand there.

"Julia mentioned that you stopped by this morning," she managed.

"You off to work?" he asked, and Emily frowned.

"Yep." Her tone was clipped but she didn't care. Something between them had shifted since last night. The spark that seemed to have been reignited in the past week was suddenly snuffed out.

She drew a breath and turned to the mailboxes. Yesterday's mail still filled their box, forgotten in the midst of everything else. Emily paused, realizing how consumed with Scott she had allowed herself to become, and then pulled the stack free from the slot, her heart lurching when she saw the thick, solid envelope with the telltale return address. She held it in her hands, blinking in disbelief, as her breath wedged in her throat.

Scott inhaled. "Free for dinner tonight?"

Emily turned her attention back to him, trying not to think of the letter in her hands, the decision she would soon be forced to make. "Sure."

"I have to go through some paperwork over at the office, but how about I swing by your place around... seven?"

Her mind immediately went to Julia, who would surely be home and who would undoubtedly get carried away with the idea of a date—Emily stopped herself. A date? Was this what it was?

"Seven will be perfect," she managed, her voice latching in her throat.

"Good, good." He nodded his head, holding her gaze, and she clung to his stare, unable to peel her eyes from him just yet. "There's something I need to tell you."

Her breath snared in her tightening chest, wondering just what he had to say, and wishing she didn't have to wait until this evening to find out.

Julia's words rushed back to her, speaking the unspoken thoughts she had harbored all those years. Maybe, just maybe, she had let him get away once. But not again. Not this time.

Before she could process what she was doing she took a step forward and carefully, slowly, clasped her lips to his. He remained still at first, but he didn't resist her, and she tried again, parting her lips to his, sighing as his tongue skimmed against her bottom lip. She felt his hand brush against her hip as the other slid behind her back and then she was against him, the hard, solid plane of his chest, her mouth clamped on his, their tongues lacing more quickly, hungry in their need. He tasted like coffee and mint toothpaste, and his hair smelled like soap. She grazed a hand down his chest, feeling the hard ripples under her fingertips and then she spread her palms to his arms. The dusting of hair against his smooth, warm skin prickled her desire on contact, and she rubbed her hands over the hard curves of his biceps.

She combed her fingers through the thick hair at the base of his neck, moaning into his mouth as he searched her with greater need, her body melting into his, and she felt in that moment that she could become his, that a part of her had always been right here in his arms, holding on to this feeling. All she needed was him—him and the sensations he aroused in her. Nothing else would matter. Not the pain he had caused her, not the loss she had endured, not her lonely child-hood. Nothing. She didn't need anything other than him. This.

Slowly, Scott pulled back, ending the kiss. "I'll see you tonight, then," he said, and Emily could only nod, frowning at the change in his expression. His smile seemed too tight. His eyes looked flat.

She waved as he slipped out onto the sidewalk and she watched his back retreat until there was nothing left to see but the slew of familiar faces passing down Main Street. He felt like a ghost again—like a person she had once held and whose memory she still clung to, but a person who had slipped away from her a long time ago.

Emily shook her head, trying to clear away the cobwebs. The envelope in her hands felt heavy—like a burden rather than the relief she had expected it to be. She stuffed it into her bag unopened and then ran as fast as she could to Sweetie Pie, and despite know-ing Lucy was waiting for her, she felt more alone than ever.

She was pinning her hopes on dreams, and she had a bad feeling they were all about to come crash-ing down.

Scott hated being at the offices of Collins Con-struction. Everything about it, from the beige Berber carpeting to the awards and plaques lining the walls, made his insides churn. The office felt like a sham—a cover for a well-preserved scandal. One of their own had died, but the company had continued, and these four walls and everything they contained felt hypo-critical. Callous. Cold.

He had once again slipped in through the back door, even though the offices were closed on the weekend. The files he needed were in his father's cabinets, and he flicked through the folders, pausing to study their contents. Scott pulled up the details of the library project, adding a few ideas here and there as he cross-referenced the blueprint spread before him. It was a shame, he knew, that such a large part of the old library had been damaged, but the reconstruction would turn the entire building into a monument, a pillar of the town. The architect had been clever with his details, ensuring the new wing would maintain the authenticity of the quaint New England town and the existing structure that hadn't been damaged, while inside, the most modern amenities would guarantee it could last long into the future. It was an important building, a community center in many ways, and despite the wall he had put up around this town, Scott couldn't help but feel a little proud to be a part of this project. It felt good to be able to do something positive for the town. For Lucy.

Scott stood up and paced the room, looking at it with fresh eyes. As a child, he used to think his father's office was enormous, but now it felt cramped and dim. The furniture he once thought so stately just looked old and worn. The room had always been like this, he supposed, but back then he just wasn't disillusioned to it yet.

On a console table near the window, Scott noticed a picture of himself wearing a hard hat and holding his father's hand. He turned it face down on the table with a scowl.

It was really time to get out of here.

Gathering a stack of files together, he grabbed his keys to leave when his sister's voice cut through the silence. "Scott!" It was a panicked cry. A cry he had heard once before, a long time ago. A cry of fear before the commotion dimmed his clarity, big men came running, shouting and his dad was grabbing him by the back of the shirt, pushing him faster than his legs could carry him until the car door slammed shut, locking him safely inside. "Scott! Scott!" His blood went still.

"Scott!" Lucy's voice sounded strangled, frozen in fear. Before he could react, she burst into the room. Her face was tearstained. Scott noticed the red rim of her eyes, the clutch of wet tissue in her hand.

"Thank God I found you," she gushed.

"What is it?" His tone was brusque, hardened in a way he hadn't intended. He was bracing himself for the worst. The anticipation was nearly choking him.

"It's Dad," Lucy whispered as her words caught in her throat. "He's been taken to the hospital in an ambulance. We have to go. Now."

He nodded abruptly. "I'll drive."

His focus remained on the back door at the end of the hall as he wove his way to it and pushed it forcefully, until it ricocheted off the back of the building. Lucy was crying harder now, explaining what had happened, if only to walk herself through it.

"I guess he passed out and hit his head on the corner of that desk near the window. I was just out there this morning, too, and he almost seemed a little better. I dared to hope..." Lucy sniffed. She hesitated before adding, "He was asking about you."

Scott ground his teeth. "That's nice," he said flatly.

"He's so proud of you, Scott," Lucy said hopefully, and Scott felt his anger begin to stir.

"Please don't, Lucy."

"Why? Why shouldn't I say something?" She almost shouted. Scott gripped the steering wheel, his mind whirling as he made a quick right at the intersection. "Why should I always have to pretend that none of this has anything to do with me? That it's only between you and them and that somehow I am just unaffected?"

"Because this *isn't* about you, Lucy," Scott said, determined to keep a clear head.

"Yes, it is! Of course it is!" Lucy insisted. "You're my brother! They're my parents! You disappeared for twelve years—twelve *years*—and now you finally come back just in time to watch Dad die! Do you know what this feels like to me? Do you, Scott? Do you even care?"

Scott kept his eyes on the road. "Of course I care."

"Then why did you have to come back and ruin everything?"

"I came back because you asked me to."

"But why couldn't you have just let things go? Why did you have to come over to the house and make everyone upset?"

Scott forced a breath, willing himself to remain calm. "I told you I shouldn't have come. You didn't listen to me."

"But—"

"But nothing, Lucy." He could no longer keep the frustration from his tone. "I didn't come over to make everyone upset. I can promise you that."

"All I wanted, all I *hoped,* was to have my family together again. I never knew what happened or why there was a rift, but I thought maybe someday… someday…" She trailed off, crying.

"Don't you think I wanted the same thing?" he asked.

"But you made it worse!" she accused.

"Maybe. Maybe so." He sighed. He certainly hadn't made it better. Scott drove on, his heart aching as her weeping filled the car. "I'm sorry you were dragged into this, Lucy."

"They wanted you to come back, you know," she hissed, fury flickering in her watery gaze. "It was you who stayed away, Scott! You tore this family apart!"

Scott fought back the mounting emotion that seized his chest. He exhaled slowly, willing himself to stay calm. "I don't expect you to understand."

"I just don't understand why you can't be the bigger person here, Scott."

"You're right, you don't understand," Scott repeated.

"Try me."

Scott slammed on the brakes at the red light and turned to lock her heated stare. He took a few breaths, and then steadied himself. "Now isn't the time," he said. "Our father is in the hospital, he's terminally ill, and I want your last image of him to be the good one you've always had. So don't make me turn you against him."

Lucy blinked. She held his gaze until the light turned green and then deflated back into her seat, crying until Scott thought he couldn't take another second of it. Had he not been punished enough? Had he not atoned for his sins? Had he not spent twelve years hating himself, wishing he could undo the irre-vocable damage? Of all the pain he had endured, this was by far the worst. He could bear the self-loathing and the sleepless nights, but listening to the hopeless cries of someone he loved and knowing there was nothing he could do to ease her pain was unbearable.

His mind immediately trailed to Emily.

As the theme song of *Passion's Crest* gained mo-mentum and Fleur studied the results of the paternity test with shaking hands, the television screen faded to black. Julia leaned back against a sofa cushion and sighed. "Fridays are such a good cliffhanger," she mused, smiling wistfully. "It was killing me to wait this long to catch up, but what choice did I have with how busy you've been lately. Out and about. Work-ing. Dating..."

"Hmm," Emily said distractedly. She had long since stopped watching the clock, but her heart still seemed to register each passing minute with a sharp pang. Nine-thirty. The only relief she could garner was knowing that Julia wasn't aware of the silent hu-miliation she was suffering all through the episode of *Passion's Crest.*

It wasn't like her to keep secrets from Julia. After all, she wasn't just her sister—she was her best friend, too. Sitting catty-corner from her now, Emily felt a wave of sadness wash over her. She wanted to just blurt out all the emotions she was keeping bottled up inside her, but for some reason she just couldn't.

Scott had stood her up. Tears stung her eyes and she held them back, feeling more angry than sad. She blinked furiously, pressing her lips tightly together.

She had only herself to be upset with now. She had dared to open her heart, and once again, he had let her down.

It was her own doing for pinning so much hope on one man. A man who had made her no promises. A man who had made it very clear that he wasn't looking for anything permanent. A man who had once told her he loved her and then disappeared.

But then, Scott's actions were never consistent with his words.

"Is everything okay?"

Emily glanced at her sister and forced a tight smile. "I'm just tired is all."

"Well, get some rest." Julia sighed, flicking off the television. "I think I'll take a shower and turn in early myself. It's been a busy weekend."

Emily walked into her room and closed the door behind her. Her heart felt heavy, like deadweight within her chest. Pulling open the top drawer of her nightstand, she fished out the letter from the culinary school, not stopping to pause as she ran her finger through the small opening and tugged free the folded piece of paper enclosed. She read the letter impassively at first, but as the meaning of the words took hold and she processed their implications, she felt her pulse begin to race.

They'd accepted her.

A tapping at the front door caused her to jump guiltily, and she quickly stuffed the letter back into the envelope and into her drawer. Opening her bedroom door, she held her breath, listening for the sound she had just heard. There it was again—she hadn't imagined it.

Emily walked through the kitchen and opened the door, gasping when she saw Scott standing in the hall. His usually broad shoulders were slumped, his ash-brown hair tousled, and his eyes... Something was wrong.

"Scott," she breathed as anger left her body. "Is everything okay?"

He shook his head. "My father's in the hospital."

"Oh, no. Is he going to be all right?"

Scott rubbed a hand over his face. His eyes were tired, and the frown seemed cemented into his squared jaw. "He's in intensive care. Lucy's there, with my mother. It's just..." He trailed off, shaking his head. "I should have called."

Emily stepped into the hall, dismissing his concerns with a wave of her hand. "No, no. I'm just sorry to hear about your dad. How are you holding up?"

He managed a hint of a smile. "Not great."

She tipped her head. "Can I do anything for you?"

He locked her gaze. "Some company would be nice."

She smiled and followed him down the hall to his room, waiting as he unlocked the door and flicked on the bedside light. The bed was made—poorly—and she recognized the stacks of paperwork and blueprints spread out on the little table where they had eaten their pie just a few nights ago.

The suitcases were still open, still prepped and ready to go.

She sat down on the bed, telling herself not to think about that now.

Scott sat next to her, close enough for their legs to touch, and stared pensively out the window. "Growing up, I always thought my father was this unbreakable force. It's not easy to see him like this."

"I can't imagine it would be. It's good you were able to come home and see him again."

"My father and I haven't spoken in twelve years," Scott said, his eyes still fixed in the distance. Emily could see his jaw twitching in his profile. "Lucy's mad at me. She thinks I should be the bigger person."

"She's just in pain," Emily said. "She just wants her family to get along, for all of you to be happy."

Scott's brow furrowed. "My father and I…I can't be sure we'll be able to make peace before it's too late."

Emily closed her eyes as her chest tightened. "You know the day my father died, he asked me to give him a kiss before he left for work, and I refused because I was angry at him for not letting me eat a piece of candy for breakfast."

Scott pulled a face. "You were just a kid. You can't take that seriously."

Emily felt the same pang of remorse she felt every time she thought of that morning. "It was all I could think about for months. For a while I wondered if I would have felt better if the last thing I said to him was 'I love you' instead of…" Tears prickled her eyes and she stopped talking.

"Do you think it would have been easier?"

"No." Emily stared at her lap. "I think we all do things we aren't proud of in life at some point or another. I can't go back and change the exchange I had with my dad that morning, but I can change the way I think about him. He wouldn't want me to live with that guilt. He'd want me to focus on everything else we shared. He'd want me to live my life to the fullest."

He'd want her to go that culinary school. She could almost see his face now when she told him the news. That broad, ear to ear grin. The pride flashing in his eyes. "That's my girl!" he'd say.

Her heart swelled until she thought it might burst. God, she missed him.

"There are a lot of things I've done that I'm not proud of, Emily."

She turned to meet Scott's heated gaze, sensing the shift in conversation. None of it mattered now. If tonight had reminded them of anything, it was that life was too short to be spent dwelling on the past.

"I know," she said, sliding her hand onto his lap to hold his hand. She squeezed his fingers as her eyes searched his face. "It's okay," she murmured softly, leaning in to graze his lips.

His tongue laced with hers, exploring her mouth with growing hunger, and she gasped at the strength of his desire as his mouth claimed hers with more greed, his hand quickly breaking her grip to slide to her waist. He pulled her close, gasping as their tongues continued their dance, and she wrapped her arms around his shoulders, pulling him close. She wanted to comfort him, but she needed to be comforted, too. She didn't know why, but somehow being touched and needed by the one person who had hurt her so much was all she needed to feel that life could go on, and that no pain lasted forever.

Gently, he pushed her back onto the bed, and she inhaled as the weight of his body pressed against hers. She ran her fingers down the length of his chest until she found his waistband and then she tugged his shirt free, tracing her fingertips ever so lightly up the smooth width of his back. His kisses became frantic, incessant in their desire, and she dragged her fingers harder down his back, clinging to him as warmth pooled in her belly.

Tearing his mouth from hers, Scott grazed his lips down her neck in tiny kisses that sent a shiver down her spine. She quivered at the lightness of his touch, the intimacy of this moment, and when her body shook he pulled her closer.

Emily gazed into his deep blue eyes, feeling more connection to him in this moment than anyone else. She held her breath as he slowly unbuttoned her blouse, and her back arched as he loosened her lace bra and met her breast with his mouth. She stifled a cry as his tongue flicked the soft flesh which budded under his touch. The feeling of his mouth on her skin and his hands on her flesh made her long for his touch all the more. She pulled his shirt over his head and then rested back against the bed, taking his bare chest in her arms, caressing his cool skin until it warmed beneath her palms.

His hands circled her abdomen and then unbuttoned her jeans. She shimmied out, freeing herself of the material that served as a barrier between their two bodies, and anticipation built as he discarded his own pants. His fingertips skimmed the line of her panties as she leaned into him, molding her flesh to his, aching to become one. She gasped as he slowly, carefully, pulled the thin material free, sliding it down her thighs with one hand as his mouth once again met hers.

Pulling himself free, he discarded his boxers and sheathed himself with a condom from his wallet. Just like high school, Emily thought with a nervous giggle. Only there wasn't anything like high school about this.

She opened her legs to him as he hovered above her, caressing the hard plane of his chest with her fingers. He locked her eyes before closing them on a kiss, stifling her moan as he entered her. She held him close, raking her hands through his hair, clutching the length of his back as he pushed deeper, the weight of his body on hers making it impossible to know where her body ended and his began. She inhaled his scent and the heat from his body, and she held him as his body shook on release.

They lay in each other's arms until their breathing had steadied, their bodies cooled. "Stay the night with me," Scott murmured, his eyelids heavy with fatigue. "Stay every night with me."

Shock slammed into her. "What?" she whispered. She waited as her pulse hammered. His eyes were closed and his chest rose and fell evenly.

She watched him sleep long into the night, finally closing her own eyes just as the first hint of morning filled the room. For so many years she had lived in a dream world, imaging what-ifs, imagining something different, better. Even sleep couldn't spare her now. Reality had come knocking, and now she had to decide what to do about it.

Chapter Ten

Emily tiptoed down the hall when dawn broke. As much as she would have loved to have remained tangled in the sheets, feeling the heavy rise and fall of Scott's chest against her back, she had to get ready for work, and she preferred to slip back into the apartment unnoticed. She enjoyed living with her sister, but there were some times when she longed for a little more privacy, and today was one of those times. She supposed if she ended up in Boston, she wouldn't have to worry anymore about Julia commenting on her whereabouts.

Her hand froze on the doorknob of her apartment as realization took hold. The letter from the culinary school. Was she even still considering it after last night? And Lucy—how could she leave Lucy in such a lurch when her father was in the hospital? As it was, Lucy was already scrambling to run both Sweetie Pie and the diner, even with George's help. How many times a day did Lucy express her appreciation, or mutter how she would be lost without Emily?

A queasiness coated Emily's stomach as she turned the handle. The apartment was thankfully still, and seeing that it was only six, Emily could only assume that Julia was still asleep. She hedged toward her bedroom, eager to seek haven behind the door, when Julia's bedroom door flung open. Startled, Emily jumped.

"My God, Julia!" she gasped, placing her hand on her heart to steady her racing pulse. "You surprised me!"

A devilish light sparked Julia's green eyes. "Well, well, well. What do we have here?" she asked, folding her arms across her chest as she leaned against the doorjamb.

Emily flashed her a warning look. "Not now, Julia." She opened the door to her own room and crossed to her closet, selecting a black skirt and top for work. "I'm running late as it is. I have to get six pies in the oven before we open at eleven."

"That's fine. I'll just talk with you while you're getting ready." Julia stood in the doorway of Emily's room now, blocking her escape.

"Please, Julia." She sighed. "Not now."

Julia narrowed her gaze but her lips twitched with a smile. "You were with Scott Collins last night, weren't you?"

"What? Why would you say such a thing?" Emily asked, but she knew it was pointless. She fumbled through her drawers mindlessly, hoping to avoid eye contact.

"Well, Sherlock, let's see... You're wearing the same clothes as last night and your bed hasn't been slept in." She tsked. "If that doesn't add up to a little hanky-panky down the hall with the mysterious blast from the past, I don't know what does."

"You really need to stop watching *Passion's Crest,*" Emily countered.

"No more than you do," Julia said lightly. Then, collapsing onto the bed, she gushed, "Oh, please tell me. Please!"

Emily stared levelly at her sister, her impatience melting into something softer. With a slow smile, she tipped her head in the direction of the hall. "I have to take a shower. Get the coffee started and I'll meet you in five minutes."

Julia squealed and shot out of the bedroom, leaving Emily standing alone in her room. She grimaced at her reflection in the mirror, wondering what Julia's reaction would be to everything. As much as she dreaded coming clean with her sister, a larger part of her would be relieved. The verdict was in, and it was time to tell Julia about the culinary school.

She showered and dressed quickly, wandering into the kitchen to pour herself a fresh cup of coffee. There were grounds at the bottom of her mug and the brew was too strong. Emily added an extra teaspoon of sugar to hide the bitter taste. Julia was dancing around excitedly, practically rubbing her hands together in anticipation, and Emily experienced a flicker of hesitation. This wasn't going to be as tantalizing as Julia expected.

"Let's sit down," she said, taking her usual chair. When Julia had settled herself she began, "Mr. Collins is in the hospital. He's been getting weaker and he fell and hit his head quite badly."

Julia's face fell. "Mr. Collins was never very nice, but it's still very sad all the same. I feel sorry for Scott." She cupped a hand to her mouth as her eyes widened. "And poor Lucy!"

"I know." Emily rubbed her forehead. "I feel horrible for her, too. Which is why I'm so conflicted."

Confusion knit Julia's brow. "Conflicted? About what?"

"This." Emily slid the acceptance letter across the table to Julia, watching as her sister silently read the single sheet of paper, her expression hovering somewhere between bewilderment and disbelief.

"I don't understand," Julia finally said, looking up. "You applied to this culinary school in Boston?" Emily nodded. "But why didn't you tell me?"

Emily winced at the twinge of hurt in her sister's voice and shrugged. "There didn't seem to be much point if I didn't get accepted. I guess I was afraid of jinxing it."

Julia stared at her, her mouth a thin line, her eyes sharp. She wasn't buying it. "You were afraid I would be upset, weren't you?"

Emily tipped her head. "I didn't know what I wanted to do, Julia. I don't want to leave you when Mom just moved away, too. But—"

"But you want something else," Julia said. "Something more."

Emily nodded. "I guess so."

Julia's mouth tipped into a slow, awestruck smile. "I

can't believe I accused you of not trying to make more
for yourself. Why didn't you tell me, then?"

"I told you, I don't know what I'm going to do."

Julia frowned. "You're going to attend this school,
that's what you're going to do."

Emily laughed softly, feeling as though she could
weep in relief. "It's not as simple as that, though. Not
anymore, at least," she added.

"Oh?" Julia said archly. "This wouldn't have something to do with Scott, would it?"

"I don't know what's happening with him," Emily
admitted, feeling lighter than she had in days now that
she could open up to someone about her innermost
fears and feelings. "I think he really cares about me,
but then I can't help thinking it will all go wrong."

"Does he know about the school?"

"No." Emily leaned across the table. "How can I
tell him? Lucy is his sister—she'll be crushed about
this, Julia. Crushed!" Her heart began to throb as she
imagined Lucy's reaction. She hated the thought of upsetting her friend right now. And Scott...could she really walk away from him now, just when she'd finally
found him again? "I'm not going," she said firmly. The
finality in her tone brought her comfort—an end to
her anxiety over the consequences of her decision—
and she said it again, with more conviction this time.
"I'm not going."

Julia held her gaze, unblinking. Her eyes were un-
readable, her expression flat, but Emily thought she
saw something there. Something that looked an awful
lot like disappointment. "All your life you've sacri-
ficed for me... Don't think I haven't noticed."

Emily felt her shoulders slump. "It wasn't a sacrifice, Julia. We're family. That's just what you do. You support each other."

"Exactly," Julia said. "And that's why I'm supporting you now. I'll be fine, Emily! And I want this for you. You obviously want it, too, or you wouldn't have applied in the first place."

Emily hesitated. "I was never sure I would really go."

"This is your chance to make something of yourself, to give yourself a whole new set of opportunities!" Julia insisted. "It wasn't a possibility for you before, but it can be now. Why wouldn't you seize this chance? Are you scared?"

Emily scoffed. "No, I'm not scared." But maybe she was. Maybe the thought of leaving her comfortable life behind was starting to feel unsettling and strange. Or maybe she was afraid of turning her back on the man she had always loved, of doing to him what he had done to her.

"Well, for what it's worth, I think you should go." Julia stood up from the table. Emily tucked the letter back into its envelope as her sister poured a mug of coffee for herself. "I think Dad would have thought the same thing," she added softly. "He wanted the best for us, and it would have saddened him to know he couldn't give it to us. This would be your way of showing him we pulled through. That we didn't miss out on things we could have had. Don't you see, Emily? You can still have the life you always wanted. You created it for yourself."

Emily smiled grimly. Leave it to her sister to always voice her own innermost sentiments. Especially the ones she was trying so hard to overlook.

* * *

It was already past eight when Scott opened his eyes to find Emily gone from his bed. For a moment the room felt still, his mind quiet. Then, like a tidal wave, it all came crashing down on him. He closed his eyes, wondering how he would get through the next twelve years as he had somehow endured the last. It was no life to live.

Deep down he had never expected to make amends with his parents, but it wasn't because he didn't want to. Somewhere within him was a need to find peace, to put the past behind them, to move on. He just wasn't sure they could find a way before it was too late.

His father had had more than twenty years to make things right for the Porter family. To take responsibility for the part his company—his son—had played in a man's death. But instead he had done nothing, kept quiet, and Scott had followed suit. At first he had done so out of horror, and fear. Of the worry of losing the only girl he'd ever loved if he told her the truth. In the years since, he had questioned his decision not to run and tell Emily everything that day. If he had told her, explained to her the part he had played in it all, would she have still loved him? Or was it better for everyone that he had left town without another word, disappeared without a trace?

Scott heaved a sigh and pushed the covers back off the bed, forcing a piece of paper onto the floor. His pulse skipped as he picked it up and read it. A note. From Emily.

His pulse quickened as he remembered the way her body had writhed beneath his. He could still feel the desire in her touch if he closed his eyes. It was a memory he would have to savor because it would never happen again. The one woman he could love forever was the one person who would soon hate him for life.

He had to tell her. Today.

For the second day in a row, Emily sold the last slice of pie an hour before closing. The demand the bakery was stirring only furthered her resolve that she should stay where she was needed. If things kept up at this pace, they'd have to double their supply. They might even need to hire a third person to cover the counter while Lucy and Emily tended to the baking.

But then, if they brought on a new person, maybe Emily wouldn't feel so bad about leaving. Lucy hadn't been to work that day, and she would probably be out for another few days more. In the brief phone call they'd had, Lucy had said her father would be in the hospital for the week at least, but that he was fortunately being moved out of the intensive care unit later that night. Now wasn't the time to make any decisions that could further distress her friend. Julia could say what she would, but Emily needed time to think about what she really wanted. What really mattered.

Still, the thought of not going to the school made her heart sink. She had only visited once as part of the admissions process, but she could still recall the way she felt when she was there. She had never felt so excited about the future—at least not since she was seventeen, dreaming about a life with Scott.

One by one, she flicked off the lights of the bakery and turned the sign on the door. The evening air was cool and refreshing, stirring up memories of long walks along the lake at the edge of town, the anticipation she would feel of long summer days and Scott's bronzed skin beside her on the rocky beach.

He was sitting on the steps leading up to the second floor apartments when Emily stepped into the vestibule. Judging from his presence, he hadn't spent the day at the hospital as Lucy had chosen to do.

"How are you doing?" Emily asked as she approached.

He gave a tight smile in return. "Feel like going for a walk?"

Emily nodded. "Sure," she said softly, waiting as he pulled himself up to standing and led her back out the door. Why couldn't she have cleaned up a bit more at the bakery? She probably had flour in her hair. She slid him a glance and realized with a pang that he probably hadn't noticed. Not necessarily a good thing, actually.

"Did you talk to my sister today?"

Emily nodded. "She told me your father was being moved into a private room. That's good news."

Scott glanced at her through hooded eyes. "It is. That was a close call last night."

They walked east on Birch Street, past the white picket fences that lined the road. A dusting of cherry blossoms showered the pavement as they approached some of her favorite houses in Maple Woods—white colonials with black shutters dating back to the eighteenth century. She knew every owner of every house, and she had been in many of them. They were good people—kind people. People she couldn't imagine leaving behind.

"There's something I should tell you, Scott." Her voice strained against the tightening in her chest.

He turned to her, his brow knitting. "What is it?"

"Do you remember the other night when you asked me if I ever considered doing something with my baking skills?" Scott nodded and she drew a sharp breath. "I wasn't completely honest with you. The truth is that I actually applied to a culinary school in Boston. I got the acceptance letter yesterday."

She lifted her eyes to his, watching as his expression brightened. "That's wonderful!" he exclaimed. His smile was broad and for a moment she felt herself get swept up in his excitement.

"But it's in Boston," she added, sobering.

He shrugged. "So?"

Emily stiffened. "So that's two hours from here."

"But it's what you always wanted, Emily. It's what I always wanted for you. To be able to live your dreams, to—"

"But we had dreams together then, Scott!"

His smile faded to a grim line. "Don't make this about me, Emily," he said.

Her heart plummeted into her stomach. So there it was. What a fool she had been.

"I wasn't planning on it," she said flatly, shifting her focus to the road. She knew he hadn't promised her anything. He had made it clear since his first day back that his visit was temporary. He had a whole life in Seattle, after all. Had she really expected him to just give it all up?

She supposed she had.

"I haven't made a decision yet so I'd appreciate if you didn't say anything to your sister. I should be the one," she said coolly. Her heart began to race with determination. She would go to that school. There was no reason not to anymore. To think she had almost given up the opportunity for Scott. She had thrown enough years away on him.

When they reached the park on Orchard Lane, Scott came to a stop. "Can we sit over there?" he asked, pointing to a wooden bench under a crab apple tree.

Heart sinking, Emily walked over to the bench. "Are you regretting last night?" she blurted before he'd even had a chance to sit down.

"What?" His brow furrowed as he ran a hand through his hair. "No, no." He sat down heavily beside her, rubbing his hand over his jaw. She could hear the soft scratching of his skin over the faint call of blue jays. "Quite the opposite," he said, his voice low and soft, and Emily felt her insides flutter.

Stay with me tonight. Stay with me forever.

Well, she had intended to do just that. Now it seemed he couldn't get rid of her fast enough. "So you don't regret it?" She frowned. "I'm sorry, Scott. I don't understand."

"Of course I don't regret it. Last night was… amazing." He huffed out a breath. "But that's just the problem, Emily," he continued.

Emily's heart sank. "What do you mean?" she asked quietly.

Scott turned to her, suddenly looking like he had aged ten years overnight. "Emily, I need to tell you something." His voice was low, barely audible, and her breath locked in her chest.

"You're scaring me."

His stare penetrated hers, reaching the depth of her heart, pulling her toward him like a magnet. She couldn't have torn her gaze from his if she wanted to.

"You always wondered why I broke things off with us."

She nodded, unable to speak from the lump in her throat.

He drew a deep breath and closed his eyes before slowly lifting his gaze to hers once more. "There was a reason."

"Okay," Emily said, encouraging him through the pause. What was done was done. She had decided to forget their past and to focus instead on their future. Their present. They were adults now, and they had something—something real—she was sure of it! In the brief amount of time since Scott had returned to town, they had formed a connection, and after last night, they had formed a bond. It couldn't be broken. Not like this. Not so quickly. Nothing he could say about that night twelve years ago could undo what they had now.

"Did anyone ever tell you the cause of your father's death?"

Emily felt like her gut was being squeezed through a vice. "What does that have to do with anything?" she replied, hearing the hysterical pitch in her voice. She didn't want to talk about her father's death or imagine the brutal way in which he had died. She'd tried to push those images from her mind a long time ago—how dare he try and bring such pain to the surface? "Why are you bringing this up? Are you trying to upset me?"

"He died on one of my father's job sites," Scott said softly.

"I know that. Of course I know that!" Emily said

sharply. She stared at him angrily. "What are you trying to tell me, Scott?"

Scott pulled his hand free of hers and raked his fingers through his hair. "They said it was human error, that he didn't pull the brakes on the machinery before stepping down into the ditch."

Well, thanks for reminding me. "Please stop," she said over her pounding heart. She could hear the blood rushing in her ears. Her legs were shaking and she pushed on her knees with both hands to still them. "I don't want to talk about this."

"It was human error, Emily, but it wasn't his."

Emily felt the blood drain from her face, and the world went quiet. She could hear nothing—not the birds in the trees, not the wind through the leaves, not the beating of her own heart.

"It was me, Emily," Scott said.

She sat paralyzed, unable to move or even blink. Scott's clenched jaw pulsed; his profile was hard and unyielding, betraying no emotion. The bastard couldn't even look her in the eye.

"I don't understand," she said calmly, her stone-cold voice unfamiliar to her own ears, as if the sound was coming from someone else, somewhere far away. It echoed from a hollow place.

Scott turned to face her, his expression full of anguish. His bright blue eyes were full of regret, full of pain. Fear knotted in her stomach as she searched his face for understanding.

"It was me, Emily! I was the one! I was on that job site that morning, climbing on machinery no kid that age should be allowed near."

She was frozen to the bench. "But the police—"

"The police were wrong, Emily! They didn't have all the facts. My dad set the stage, he got me out of there. It was easy for them to just assume what he told them was correct. There was no evidence to the contrary."

"I don't understand." Her voice was shrill. She reflexively pulled back on the bench, desperate to distance herself from him. From his words. "I don't understand."

"It was me, Emily! Me! I got in the way. I was climbing on the machine. I left it in gear before I climbed off, and…it rolled. It was an accident, but—" His voice broke on the last word. "I wasn't even aware of what I did, Emily. I was a stupid little kid. But… I'm to blame for your father's death."

He had feared this moment for twelve long years. He had rehearsed his words, anticipated her reaction and played out every possible scenario until he was in a cold sweat. He hadn't planned on this. He couldn't have.

Emily sat on the bench, unmoving. Her creamy skin had paled to a ghostly white. She wasn't crying or screaming or shouting that she hated him. She was just sitting there. Shaking.

Words he could deal with, but silence was something he was unprepared for. He watched her guardedly, waiting for her to speak, to do something. He ran his hands down his face; his head was pounding. What did she want from him? What did she want him to do? He would do anything in that moment if he knew it would make her feel better. He would get up and leave. He would take her into his arms.

He reached out a hand but she pushed it away before it could reach her. Her eyes were narrowed and sharp. "Don't touch me."

"Okay," he said. He heaved a breath and tented his fingers on his lap.

"How long have you known?" she asked. Her voice was barely above a whisper. Her eyes were focused somewhere in the distance and he followed her gaze to a little bird pecking at a bruised and fallen apple.

"Since the night I left town." He paused. "I was always fooling around on equipment, running around my father's job sites. I never knew until my parents told me, until I heard them talking—I never knew the part I had played."

"You were there that day."

He nodded. "Yes."

"And you don't remember?"

"All I remember is playing on the machines, hopping off. Then suddenly there was all this shouting, and next thing I knew my dad was grabbing me, telling me to get away." He drew a sharp breath. "My last night in town, I overheard my parents arguing about it. When I confronted them, they told me. For nine years they'd kept me from knowing it had been my doing."

"And you kept it from me for another twelve," she murmured. "Is that why you left Maple Woods?"

Scott nodded as shame weighed heavily in his heart. "Yes." He regarded her carefully before adding, "I didn't want to hurt you any more than I already had. I thought it was better that way."

"And now?" She turned a sharp gaze on him. Accusation flashed in her gray eyes.

He hadn't been expecting that one. He searched for

the right words, anything that might ease her pain. "I'm older now. I've had time to think. I couldn't live with myself anymore."

"Do you feel better now?"

Her words were a punch to the gut. "No."

She held his eyes miserably, her expression withering as a tear released. She brushed it away quickly with a sniff, turning her attention back to the little bird. "Who else knows?"

"No one," Scott began and then halted. "Except my parents. That's why I stopped speaking to them. When they told me what had happened, what they had kept from me—" he glanced at her "—and you…I couldn't forgive them."

Emily jaw flinched but her profile held unwavering stoicism. "Not Lucy?"

"Not Lucy." He drew a breath and reached into his pocket and handed her the folded check.

"What's this?" Emily asked, taking it.

"It's what your family should have had a long time ago," Scott said quietly, watching as Emily unfolded the check and stared at the number.

Wordlessly, she handed it back to him. "I don't want this."

He scanned her face, frowning. "Emily, take it. It's what your family deserved. It would have made your lives easier. Better."

"Better. You think my life is better now, knowing this, knowing you kept this from me? What was this week all about, Scott? A way to ease your guilt? A way to make up for breaking my heart? A way to make up for—" Her voice cracked and she shook her head, lowering her eyes. Sitting at the end of the bench, she might as well have been sitting across the park or across the town. Across the country. He had never felt more helpless or more incapable of reaching out and just touching her.

"You have no idea how much I care about you, Emily," he said with quiet force.

She shook her head furiously, releasing a bitter laugh. "Yeah, right."

"Emily." He was pleading now, and he didn't care. "I mean it. Just tell me what you want me to do. Is there anything I can do?"

She nailed him with a look of scorn. Her tears had dried, her eyes reflecting something far worse than sadness. "Anything you can do?"

Her tone cut him deep. "It was a stupid question."

She scowled. "You never should have come back."

He swallowed hard. So there it was. Worst-case scenario. She hated him. Had he really ever expected anything different? His chest felt like lead as he nodded slowly, resigning himself to the consequences of his actions. "I'll go. I'll go tonight."

"I think that's a good idea," she said, her tone turning his breath to ice. She stood and walked calmly away without so much as a look back. His eyes never left her until she was completely out of sight. It was the last time he would ever see her and he had to hold on to her right up until the very last second.

Chapter Eleven

It was time to leave Maple Woods. For good this time. There were just a few more things to take care of and he could catch the red-eye to Seattle.

The sadness in Emily's eyes was a memory he would have to live with forever, but he told himself it was better than leaving again without telling her. A niggling of doubt began to creep through his mind, causing his gut to stir uneasily. He had done the right thing, even if it had opened old wounds—hadn't he? Emily deserved the truth. Mr. Porter deserved to have his family know that his death had not been a result of his own careless error.

Scott walked slowly through town, past Sweetie Pie and Lucy's Place, past the town square where a few nights ago he and Emily had danced together. His mind filled with an image of Emily framed by the glow of the lights hanging from the trees, stepping toward him under the umbrella of the leaves, her lips curving into a smile as he took her in his arms and twirled her to the beat of the music.

He'd never forget that smile.

The lights were on in Lucy's house, and he climbed the stairs to her front porch slowly, prolonging the moment when he would say goodbye to her again, when her opinion of him would change forever. If he didn't say something to her, Emily surely would.

Before he could turn and run from his problems again, he forced himself to knock loudly on the door. He peered through the long window frame until his sister appeared. She hesitated when she saw him, drawing a breath before she approached the door.

"Good of you to come," she said, struggling to meet his gaze.

Scott frowned. "How are you?"

Lucy looked around the room, seeming to try to hide from his question. "Not good, Scott."

Of course she wasn't good. He didn't even know why he'd asked. "I'm sorry, Lucy. If there's anything I can do—"

She snapped her eyes to his. "Are you going to stop by the hospital again? Dad's awake, and I'm sure he'd appreciate a visit from his only son."

From the briskness in her tone and the defensive lift of her chin, he suspected she already knew the answer. "I'm heading out of town tonight, actually."

A bitter burst of laughter escaped from her lips. "Of course you are."

Scott ignored his sister's biting tone and crossed into the living room. "We need to talk," he said firmly.

His blood felt thick and cold. There was no going back now.

Lucy hesitated, sensing the change in his mood. "What's going on?" she asked, her brow furrowing. She looked tired and worn-down. Her hair was pulled back in a loose knot and her face was pale and wan.

It killed him to do this to her but she had to know. Now. Before he left for good.

He motioned to the sofa near the window. "Can we sit down?"

Lucy bristled. "I have a lot to do before I get back to the hospital, Scott. Can this wait until after visiting hours, or will you already be halfway to Seattle by then?"

"This can't wait." He grimaced at the sharp edge to his voice, watching as his sister's eyes darkened. Her brow furrowed as she took a seat at the edge of the sofa. She looked impatient and restless, and more than a little curious.

Scott averted his gaze from the handful of framed photos Lucy kept on the mantle, unable to look at the face of the man who had determined his path and who had selfishly put their family above all others. Too restless to sit, he gripped the back of a wing chair as his gut tensed with emotion. There was no time for sentimentalities now. It would only make this more difficult than it already was.

"Scott?" He looked down to meet her stricken face. "What is going on, Scott?"

Dragging this out wasn't an option. "Do you really want to know the truth? Why I left all those years ago? Why I couldn't forgive Dad?"

Lucy looked on the verge of tears. "Of course I do,"

she said. "But—maybe I should let it go. What's done is done. It's too late."

"It's not too late," Scott said sharply. He heaved a sigh, steadying himself. "It's not too late," he repeated more calmly. "We have to make things right when we still have the chance. And that's what I've decided to do."

"What are you trying to say?"

"It shouldn't have gone on for so long." He swallowed. "The night I left home, I discovered something that I couldn't live with."

Lucy's frown deepened. She nodded. "Go on."

"Everyone always said that Mr. Porter died by his own carelessness. That he forgot to pull the emergency brake on the excavator, that human error caused it to roll over him."

Lucy stared at him in confusion. "Richard Porter? Emily's father?" Lucy's brow rose. "Scott, why are you even bringing this up?"

He held up a hand. "Mr. Porter's death was an accident. But I was the one who caused it."

Lucy stared at him in disbelief. Scott held his breath against the silence of the room. "I don't know what you're talking about," she said calmly.

Scott sighed, burdened by the need to repeat himself, to confirm the horrible circumstances. "I was on the job site that day," he explained. "Just like I always was in my spare time as a kid. And I was the last person on the machine before it rolled down into the ditch."

Lucy was staring at him with an intensity he had never seen before. She didn't blink. "You remember this?"

"No!" He combed his hair off his forehead, stared into his hands. "I was nine years old. That day was a blur to me. I just remember climbing on the equipment, running around in the dirt, and then the screams. The frantic way Dad grabbed me and thrust me into your car, hissing at us to go straight home and to never say a word if questioned."

Lucy nodded. "Right. I remember that, too."

"But I heard Mom and Dad talking the night I left town. They were talking about it, Lucy. They were talking about that day, and what happened. They kept it a secret from me for nine years. That's why they never liked Emily. That's why…why I couldn't be with her after I found out."

She leaned forward. Her eyes looked wild, her face was a chalky-white. "They said *you* caused the accident?"

Scott nodded. "Yes!"

Lucy stared at him wordlessly, and then finally relaxed against the couch. Her mouth was parted, but no sound came out, until finally she said, "I'm sorry, Scott. But that's not what happened that day at all. I was there. I was dropping off sandwiches for Dad's lunch when it all happened. I'd just finished putting them in the trailer when the shouts rang out and Dad started yelling for me to get back in the car and go, to take you home. I was there, Scott. And in the chaos of everything, no one bothered to ask me what I saw."

The timer to the oven buzzed. Right on time, Emily thought with a small smile. The test of a true baker was being able to know when a pie was done by the smell, and by the scent of cinnamon and apples wafting through the kitchen, instinct told Emily this was going to be one good deep-dish pie. Almost good enough to fill that hole in her heart.

She placed the dish on the cooling rack and closed the oven door with her hip. With hands already coated in flour, she rolled fresh dough into a large circle and then carefully positioned it in a glass pie plate. The comfort of the routine distracted her, and she felt her shoulders relax as she filled the shell with the fruit mixture from her large ceramic bowl. She took care in spreading the filling evenly with the back of her wooden spoon. A sprinkling of brown sugar would add a nice flavor under the second crust, she decided on a whim.

Crimping the edges together, she took small pleasure in the well-honed skill, remembering the way her mother had first taught her to squeeze the crusts between her thumb and forefinger. It was comforting and peaceful to work with her hands—a constructive way to work through the grief.

She carefully set the pie in the oven and turned the timer. The kitchen was a mess and she huffed in dismay as she tossed a dish towel over her shoulder. There was only one issue she took with baking: cleaning up afterward.

Still, cleaning was better than wallowing in pity and eating her way through half a gallon of fudge ripple ice cream. The past week had been a whirlwind of emotions, and it would take some time to get back on track. If she could focus on the normal routine of her day, then she should be okay. Someday.

In a way, she should probably be relieved. After all, for years she had held on to the pain Scott had caused her when he dumped her without a word. Now she could at least scratch that ridiculous sentiment off her list. To think she had been so shattered over something so...trivial! In light of the damage Scott had really caused her, it seemed almost laughable that she should have ever been so upset over a teenage romance that never led to anything more. There was no room for pining now. Last night had been an illusion. An experience built on hopes and dreams. And lies.

For twelve years he had hidden this secret from her—from everyone!—all this time knowing that her father hadn't died by his own careless error, the way everyone in town believed.

It was wrong, and so very unfair that this was all they remembered him by. And it wasn't even true! Deep down she had never believed it—her father was good at his job, he took pride in it, but she knew her mother lost sleep about it, and she could still remember her mutterings at the funeral. He had worked too hard. He was tired. Worn-out. Maybe...

The thought of her mother that day haunted her almost as much as the memory of her father's grin, the way he would swoop her and Julia into his arms each night when he came home, as if they were weightless. He'd lift them up and somehow, with his support, it was as if they could fly.

And now she alone knew the truth. She would have to tell her mother, and Julia. She would have to bear that responsibility, brace herself for their reaction.

Emily bit her lip as she scraped the pie filling from the wooden spoons. She would not think of the pain in Scott's eyes. She would not think of the remorse in his tone. The anguish—*no*.

Tears prickled her eyes. She quickly blinked them away as she heard a key turn in the lock and her sister appeared.

"Hey there!" Julia smiled brightly and plopped her bag down on the table with a heavy thud. She glanced around the dirty-dish-strewn kitchen, eyes gleaming as she spotted the pie. "Oh, yum! Or…" A wave of disappointment crossed her face. "For Sweetie Pie?"

"For you," Emily said impulsively. She could always make another tonight. God knew she wouldn't be finding sleep, and keeping busy was better than dwelling on her own misery.

Julia's face brightened. "Really?" she said, already grabbing a plate from the cabinet. "Should I get one for you?"

Emily shook her head. "I get enough at work," she fibbed. She pressed her hand to her stomach. It had churned itself raw. She wasn't sure she would ever have an appetite again. With a tight smile she cautioned, "You might want to let it cool a bit first."

"Oh, pshaw." Julia sliced a large wedge and eagerly cracked the crust with her fork. "Delicious," she said when she had swallowed the first bite. "You really do have a gift, Em. I'm not just saying it to be nice, either. You know I'm honest to a fault."

"Thanks." Emily turned her back and lifted the faucet handle to soak the dirty mixing bowls.

Julia leaned a hip against the counter. "So have you given any more thought to that school?"

Her chest felt heavy. She had given quite a bit of thought to it, but her emotions weren't to be trusted just now. Her judgment felt clouded. "I'm still thinking about it," she said evenly.

"Did you talk to Scott about it?"

Emily closed her eyes. "Julia." She sighed.

"Well, don't let him be the deciding factor, Emily," Julia said. "Promise me that much at least. If there's something between you, he can wait. There are some things in life you have to do for yourself, Emily. Not for me. Not for Mom. Not for Scott."

Emily turned around to face her sister and wiped her hands on a nearby dish towel. She felt weary, but she knew if she went to bed and closed her eyes she would just be haunted by demons she didn't want to face. "What about Lucy? She's depending on me."

"You've done nothing but take care of us since Daddy died," Julia said. "Don't you think it's time for you to do something for yourself? I know how much you care about Lucy—she's a great friend to all of us—but she can take care of herself. She would want this for you, Emily. She sees your talent! Don't hold yourself back. It's too big of an opportunity."

Emily held her sister's gaze. She couldn't hold back the truth any longer. As tempting as it was to shelter Julia as much as she had tried to all her life, keeping this information from her sister would make her just as guilty as Scott.

"Julia." She stopped. "Can we talk for a minute?"

Julia frowned and then took another bite of pie. "We are talking."

Emily hesitated. "It's about something else. Something…serious."

Julia set her fork down, her expression sobering. Immediately Emily wished she could have kept her mouth shut. In a matter of seconds she was going to shatter her sister's world, tear open wounds that had never properly healed and now never could.

"What is it?"

Emily tipped her chin in the direction of the cramped living room and they silently settled into their usual spots. Unable to make eye contact, Emily stared into her lap. "It's about Dad. It's about what happened to him."

She waited for Julia to say something, but for once, her sister was speechless. There was no turning back.

"The accident wasn't Dad's fault," she said.

"Then whose was it?" Julia demanded quickly.

Emily pressed her lips together. "It was Scott's fault."

The room went still. Emily wasn't even sure she could feel her own pulse. She waited for Julia to speak, to say something, but she couldn't be sure her sister was breathing, either.

"Scott?" Julia finally said. "But how—"

"He told me. Today." Emily gave her sister a level stare. Julia's eyes were so wide, Emily could make out the whites around her green irises, which had darkened to mud. "He was nine years old and he was the last one on the…" She couldn't bring herself to say the word. "He didn't know it was his fault. And when he found out, nine years later, he left town."

"He didn't know until then? No one told him?"

Emily shook her head. "He didn't realize what he had done, that he was to blame. His parents covered it up. As a result, we didn't get a dime of insurance money."

"Oh, my God," Julia groaned. "I didn't even think

of that part. Not that money could have brought Daddy back."

"No." Emily's voice was clipped. Anger was setting in. "No, but it would have made Mom's life a heck of a lot easier."

Julia nodded. Her expression was pained as she stared to the far wall. The temperature had dropped with the setting sun and an evening breeze flew in the half-open windows. Emily shivered.

"Poor Scott," Julia said, and Emily felt her jaw drop.

"What?"

"Poor Scott," Julia said, searching her face. "He loved you so much, Emily. And then he found out what his parents did—"

"What *he* did," Emily reminded her. Her chest was heaving with emotion. What the hell was Julia thinking?

"But he didn't know. It was his father's fault for allowing a kid on a construction site!" Julia leaned forward. "My God, Emily. What was he supposed to do? Run and tell you then and there? He was torn between you and his parents! And finding out what he had done—" She broke off, shaking her head. "It must have torn him apart! It must have driven him nearly *mad!*"

"You're getting carried away with that ridiculous soap opera again, Julia!" Emily snapped. She silently vowed to stop watching *Passion's Crest* for good.

"No," Julia said. Her tone was firm enough to make Emily sit up a little straighter. "No, Emily, this is reality. Real life. Yours, mine. Scott's. Think of what he's carried with him all these years."

"He should have told me," Emily insisted.

"And what would you have said if he had? Huh?" Julia cocked her head. "If he had told you twelve years ago what he had done, how would you have reacted?"

Emily frowned. She shook her head, searching for an answer. It didn't matter. It didn't matter what she would have said. "I don't know," she said.

"It took a lot of courage for him to tell you, Emily. He ran away because he loved you, because he didn't want to hurt you. And he told you the truth now, after all these years, because he still loves you. And because he knows you deserved to hear it."

A painful knot had wedged itself in her throat, but Emily willed herself not to cry. What did it matter if Scott loved her then or loved her now? It didn't change anything. Not a damn thing. But for some reason, it did matter. It mattered an awful lot.

Scott stared at his sister in disbelief. "I don't understand. Mom and Dad said that it was me—my fault."

Lucy shook her head forcefully. "No. No, I was there. I remember, because I was worried you were going to slip climbing off that machine. It was parked right at the edge of that ditch, and it made me nervous."

"Rightfully so," Scott said grimly.

"You started walking around, picking up nails. You were always collecting little things like that."

Scott rested his elbows on his knees, leaning forward. "But what happened then?"

"Right after you hopped off the machine, Richard Porter climbed back on. He moved the machine an inch, then cursed, like he'd forgotten something. It was the curse that caught my attention." She frowned deeply, as if reliving the moment all over again. "And then he jumped down into the ditch, and the next thing I knew…"

"The excavator rolled," Scott finished for her.

Lucy closed her eyes. "Yes," she said softly.

Scott dragged a hand down his face. "So it really was Mr. Porter's fault?"

"But Dad thought it was you?" She sighed. "It all happened so fast. You must have been the last one he saw on the machine before it happened. And he just assumed." Urgency flared in Lucy's eyes. "You have to speak with Emily."

Scott's pulse was racing. He pressed his lips together, fighting that war of emotions that waged within him. "It's too late," he huffed. She wouldn't want to hear it. She had told him to leave town. To never come back. "What am I supposed to do, just go knock on her door?"

Lucy widened her gaze, driving home the obvious. "Yes. That's exactly what you should do."

"And tell her it was her father's error all along? That's going to go down nicely." He pounded a fist against his thigh. He didn't know which outcome was worse. "Lucy, maybe it really was my fault—"

She looked at him with pity. "No, Scott. I saw. I remember it clear as day. Who would be able to forget something so awful? You hopped off and Mr. Porter climbed on. He moved the machine. He was the last one operating it. It…it was just a tragic accident."

Scott released a long sigh, dragging his eyes over to the photos that lined the mantle in silver frames. His eye caught one of their trips to Martha's Vineyard when he was about eight. It was a black-and-white photo, glossy enough to have been torn from a magazine. Happy enough, too. His hair was lighter then and his teeth were crooked. Lucy stood beside him with a mouthful of braces, sporting a hairstyle that was popular back then but which probably made her cringe now. His parents stood behind them, tanned and young.

It was before the accident. Before their lives were shattered forever. After that day, his father became distant and removed, and his mother had a tired look about her. Nothing was ever the same again.

Scott shifted his gaze back to his sister. "She'll still think I lied to her, Lucy. It doesn't change anything."

"Yes, it does," Lucy urged. She reached over and set a hand on his wrist. Her eyes were pleading, but he didn't want to believe her. He didn't want to hope. "Go to her, Scott. For me."

He managed a tight smile. "I'm always doing favors for you."

"Good, because I have one more." She paused. "Find forgiveness in your heart for Dad, Scott. He thought he was protecting you. He made a bad decision—a bunch of bad decisions, honestly—but it wasn't black-and-white. He thought he was taking the path that would cause the least amount of damage. For you. For us. For all the other people that depended on their jobs with the company. It doesn't make it right, but he was trying to survive a horrible situation. Please try to understand that."

Scott gritted his teeth. "I'm not there yet, Lucy."

"I'm just saying that I understand the lengths people will take to protect their loved ones," Lucy said and they both knew she was referring to Bobby's involvement in the destruction of the town library. "That's all Dad was trying to do. In his heart, he thought he was protecting you."

Scott nodded slowly. "I'll stop by the hospital tonight. But first…I have to see Emily."

He tried to dismiss the uncertainty that filled him as he hugged his sister goodbye and walked through the door, a much freer man than when he had entered. There was a chance that Emily wouldn't care what he had to say. The truth was one thing. Trust was another.

He strode around the corner, toward the doorway to the apartments above the diner. The key felt heavy in his hand. This was his last chance. His last chance to win back the woman who had somehow found the way to his heart, and who would forever hold a place in it.

Emily had just taken another pie out of the oven when she heard the knock. She froze, bent over at the waist, oven mitt gripping the side of the scalding pie plate, her breath locked tight in her chest.

It was him. She knew it was him. The only other person it could be was Lucy, and Lucy would have called first.

But what more could he possibly want from her now? Hadn't he said enough for one day?

Maybe if she was quiet enough he would think she wasn't home and go away. Maybe he would turn and walk back down the stairs and climb into that flashy red sports car and speed out of town. Out of her life the way he had twelve years ago. She'd never see him again and eventually…well, eventually she would forget him.

So why did her heart feel so heavy at the thought?

Slowly, she stood, listening over the sound of her own shallow breaths. He was still there. Even through the door she could sense his presence. He knocked again. Louder this time. Why was he so determined? Why couldn't he just let her go?

Emily set the pie on the stovetop with a thud and untied her apron strings. Inhaling deeply for courage, she walked to the door and opened it. Scott stared back at her. And damn if she didn't want to just fall into his arms right then and there, go back to that magical place they had been in only the night before. *Stay with me forever,* he'd said.

She bit back on her teeth. He had known then. Known when he'd spoken those words. Known that he was lying to her.

"You're still here."

Scott blinked. "I'm heading out of town tonight, just as you asked."

Emily hoped the disappointment wasn't evident on her face. She tucked the emotion back into place. She was holding on to an illusion, a hope for what could have been. Not what was.

"But I need to talk to you before I go." His tone was urgent and quick.

"I think you've said about enough for one day, Scott."

"Emily, please. I wouldn't be here if it wasn't important."

Down the hall, Emily could make out the sound of Julia's door opening, and she stepped out into the hall, closing the apartment door behind her. "I don't know why I'm agreeing to this," she said, folding her arms tightly across her chest.

"I know why you're agreeing to it," he said, and her eyes widened in surprise. "Because you love me, Emily. And I love you. I always have. I—" His voice broke off. "I always will."

Her heart skipped a beat. She didn't need to hear this. She didn't want to hear this. It was hard enough already. Scott's admittance had seared open wounds much deeper than his betrayal, of the loss of her first love. Over and over she played out the circumstances of her father's death; the horrible, pitying look people would give her mother, Julia, her. "You certainly have a strange way of showing it," she said tightly.

Scott huffed out a breath. He took a step closer to her. She took a step back.

"Please—"

"Don't deny what we've shared these past few days. All these years later, there's still something between us."

Emily struggled to meet his eyes. "Maybe so, but it's not enough."

"Yes, it is. For me, at least. You're the one, Emily. I let circumstances tear us apart once before, and I'll be damned if I let it happen again."

She looked at him sharply. "What do you mean?"

"Emily, twelve years ago I was scared. I was shocked. And I was...I was horrified, Emily. For a dozen years I have done nothing but think of you. The guilt has nearly destroyed me."

She snorted. Raking her eyes down his fine physique, she quipped, "Could have fooled me." But even as she spoke, she felt ashamed of herself, uncertain. Julia's words came rushing back to her, and she thought of that eighteen-year-old boy who had made her a picnic in Central Park and who held her books every day after school. The boy whose blue eyes sparked with each grin, and the way that grin never faded when he was with her. And she thought of how it must have felt to have learned that he had hurt the person he loved so much.

Because he really had loved her. Once.

"I just had a long talk with Lucy," Scott said. His eyes were locked on hers, their intensity so penetrating she wanted to look away, but she couldn't. "Emily. Emily, it wasn't me. I wasn't responsible."

She felt the blood drain from her face. "Excuse me?"

"Lucy was there that day, and no one knew she'd seen what happened, no one ever questioned her. It was— Emily, I'm sorry. She confirmed the story. The events that were officially reported were the true events."

She blinked. "You mean the false report your father gave?"

"No." Scott dragged out a breath. "My father was trying to protect me, yes. But Lucy saw the entire thing. And my father ordered her to drive me home, so no one knew I was there. Or her. She couldn't give a statement. She couldn't report what she'd witnessed."

Understanding took hold as she held his gaze, saw the sadness in his eyes, the pain this was causing him.

"It was human error," she said softly. "My father's error."

Scott took a step toward her. "I'm sorry, Emily. Lucy's downstairs, if you want to talk to her."

Emily pulled away. She frowned at the floor, trying to process this turn of events. "No. No, if Lucy said that is what she saw, then I believe her." She met his eyes. "Lucy would never lie to me."

"I'm sorry I hurt you. Then. Now. It was the one thing I wanted to avoid. I only ever wanted to protect you. If I thought it would have been better to take the blame myself, I would have left tonight."

"Why didn't you?"

"Because I love you, Emily. I always have. I always will. I couldn't leave town again without making sure that this time I took the risk and told you the truth."

Emily bit on her lip, considered his words. When she looked up at him, she saw a shadow of the man she saw that first day he had strolled into the Sweetie Pie Bakery. Gone was the confident prodigal son who had swept into town. In his place was the man who had been burdened with this secret for twelve years. Even now, even when he had been vindicated, he was still turning to her to set him free.

"I'm not leaving tonight, Emily." He took another step toward her, and this time she didn't recoil. "I'm not going to lose you twice in one lifetime."

Her heart skipped a beat. "You really mean that? You're staying in Maple Woods?"

He nodded. "But I want you to go to that school. I want you to live the life you always wanted."

She tipped her head as a slow smile crept over her mouth. "This is the life I always wanted, Scott. You and me. Just the way it should have always been."

"But you had so many dreams. I thought I stole them from you once. I won't be the one to take an opportunity from you now."

Emily nodded slowly. "I won't give up that dream. I do want to go to school, but there are closer options. Before I wanted to run away from Maple Woods and start over. Now, I'm right where I want to be."

He grinned ruefully. "I know the feeling."

She nodded. "We share a lot, Scott."

"Too much to get past?" He cocked a brow.

She beamed. "Enough to build on."

Epilogue

Emily's eyes widened as she watched Scott attempt to lift the pie crust off the marble work top. The edges were jagged and there was a definite hole in the center, and she could tell from where she stood at the end of the kitchen island that the dough was much too thick and should have been rolled longer.

Scott's forehead was creased in concentration as he arranged the crust over the filling, attempting to stretch it to reach the edges of the plate and inadvertently causing another tear, which he simply pinched back together with his thumb and forefinger.

Emily laughed; she couldn't help it.

"You're laughing now," Scott said, glancing in her direction, "but trust me, by the end of the night you'll be saying this is the best pie you've ever eaten."

She arched a brow. "Oh, will I?"

"Wait and see," he teased, sliding the pie plate off the counter and putting it into the hot oven. "You might be the one in culinary school, but this is one recipe you're never going to forget."

"Oh, I have no doubt about that," Emily said.

Emily shook her head as Scott stood before the oven, staring through the glass, waiting for the pie to bake. "You're going to be waiting for a pretty long time," she said, setting her hands on her hips.

"What can I say?" he asked, turning around with a suggestive grin. "The best things in life are worth waiting for."

She kissed him softly on the mouth, beaming at the compliment, and then commented, "When you said you wanted me to teach you how to make a pie, I didn't realize I was dealing with such a confident pupil."

"You've been working hard lately," Scott said, taking the rag from her hand. He wiped the flour off the counter and took the mixing bowl and wooden spoon to the sink. "Between working here and driving over to Hartford for your classes three times a week, I figured it would be nice for someone else to do the cooking for a change."

She tried to hide the skepticism in her expression. From the corner of her eye she could the see the pie filling already oozing through the lumpy crust, hissing as it hit the hot oven rack. She bit back a sigh. She'd have to clean the oven before they left tonight; Lucy wouldn't appreciate walking into Sweetie Pie in the morning and finding one of her ovens covered with the sticky remnants of Scott's baking efforts.

"I do have a bit of homework for tomorrow," Emily admitted.

Scott grinned. "Perfect. You do that while I clean up this mess. Trust me, Em. You're in for the surprise of your life."

Emily laughed softly as she glanced at the oven again. Oh, she didn't have any doubt about that.

An hour later, the buzzer went off and Emily looked up from her notebook just as Scott was pulling his pie from the oven. If he noticed the way the berry filling had exploded onto the top crust, staining it red, he didn't seem to mind any more than he did about the strange way the crust hung over one edge of the plate and didn't quite reach the other.

"What do you think?" he asked, flashing her a smile that lit his eyes.

"It's the most beautiful pie I've ever seen," Emily had to say, because in many ways it was. He'd made it with his own two hands, just for her. It didn't get more perfect than that. "Maybe we should let it cool first," she suggested, but Scott just waved away her concern.

"Stay here," he instructed as he slipped through the kitchen door.

A moment later he returned, looking considerably less confident than he had only minutes earlier. His blue eyes were a notch brighter, but they studied her with newfound interest, as if gauging her every reaction. She made a mental note to eat every last bite of the pie, no matter what it tasted like. She had experience, after all, from when Julia decided to contribute to meals.

She crossed the room and took Scott's hand, noticing the way he gripped hers ever so slightly tighter than usual. He moved slowly, too, as if savoring the moment, and finally pushed open the door with his free hand.

Emily gasped. Somehow, in the time they had been in the kitchen, Sweetie Pie had been transformed. Hundreds of translucent pink balloons hung from the ceiling, and the entire room glowed from the flickering votive candles lined along the glass display case. A path of pink rose petals led to the only table remaining, with Scott's pie resting proudly in the center.

She walked slowly, taking it all in, sliding a shy smile to Scott, who was watching her carefully, eager for her approval. "Lucy helped," he whispered. "Do you like it?"

"Like it? This is…" She trailed off, turning to take in the entire room, and then looked up to meet Scott's nervous grin. He was staring at her with an intensity she hadn't seen before.

Her stomach dropped as she realized what was happening. What this all meant. What he had been up to.

"Emily." Scott's voice was low and deep, but never more certain. He reached down and took her other hand in his, throwing her that lopsided grin that made her heart turn over.

"Oh, my God." Her pulse was racing, and she could feel the tears welling in her eyes.

She watched in slow motion as he dropped to one knee and looked up at her, his smile never faltering, his hands warm and strong as they clung to hers. They'd found each other in this room, after twelve long years, and soon she would have the certainty of knowing they would never be apart again. She stared into the eyes of the boy who had held umbrellas over her head on those rainy walks home from school, who had met her with an eager smile on those lazy summer evenings when she could spend hours lying in the cool grass, listening to the smooth sound of his voice, and she saw the man she was going to spend the rest of her life with. And she knew then and there that he was right: that the recipe he had cooked up for her tonight was the best one she could have ever imagined. Lumpy pie and all.

* * * * *

Available April 15, 2014

#2329 THE PRINCE'S CINDERELLA BRIDE
The Bravo Royales • by Christine Rimmer

Lani Vasquez cherishes her role as nanny to the Montedoran royal children—particularly since it offers proximity to her good friend, the handsome Prince Maximilian. Max has grieved his lost wife for years, but this Prince Charming is ready for the next chapter of his love story—and his Cinderella is right under his nose.

#2330 FALLING FOR FORTUNE
The Fortunes of Texas: Welcome to Horseback Hollow
by Nancy Robards Thompson

Christopher Fortune has gladly embraced the wealth and power of his newfound family name. But not everyone's as impressed by the Fortune legacy. His new coworker, Kinsley Aaron, worked for everything she ever got, and Chris's newly entitled attitude rubs her the wrong way. Now Chris will have to earn Kinsley's love—and his Fortune fairy-tale ending....

#2331 THE HUSBAND LIST
Rx for Love • by Cindy Kirk

Great job? Check. Hunky hubby? Not so much. Dr. Mitzi Sanchez has her life just where she wants it—except for the husband she's always dreamed of. She creates a checklist for her perfect man—but she insists pilot Keenan McGregor isn't it. With a bit of luck, Keenan might blow Mitzi's expectations sky-high....

#2332 HEALED WITH A KISS
Bride Mountain • by Gina Wilkins

Both burned by love, wedding planner Alexis Mosley and innkeeper Logan Carmichael aren't looking for anything serious when they plunge into a passionate affair. Little by little, though, what starts as a no-strings-attached fling evolves into something much deeper. Can they heal their emotional wounds to start afresh, or will the ghosts of relationships past haunt them forever?

#2333 GROOMED FOR LOVE
Sweet Springs, Texas • by Helen R. Myers

Due to her declining sight, Rylie Quinn abandoned her dreams of becoming a veterinarian and moved to Sweet Springs, Texas, as an animal groomer. She just wants to get on with her life—something that irritating attorney Noah Prescott won't allow her to do. He's determined to dig up Rylie's past, and, as he and Rylie butt heads, true love might just rear its own.

#2334 THE BACHELOR DOCTOR'S BRIDE
The Doctors MacDowell • by Caro Carson

Bright, free-spirited and bubbly, Diana Connor gets under detached cardiologist Quinn MacDowell's skin...and not in a way he'd care to admit. When the two are forced to work together at a field clinic, Quinn begins to see just how caring Diana is and how well she interacts with patients. This heart doctor might just need a bit of Diana's medicine for himself....

YOU CAN FIND MORE INFORMATION ON UPCOMING HARLEQUIN® TITLES, FREE EXCERPTS AND MORE AT WWW.HARLEQUIN.COM.

HSECNM0414

REQUEST YOUR FREE BOOKS!
2 FREE NOVELS PLUS 2 FREE GIFTS!

⟨H⟩ HARLEQUIN®

SPECIAL EDITION

Life, Love & Family

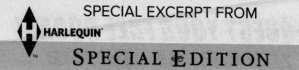

Lani Vasquez is a nanny to the royal children of Montedoro...and nothing more, or so she thinks. But widower Prince Maximilian Bravo-Calabretti hasn't forgotten their single passionate encounter. Can the handsome prince and the alluring au pair turn one night into forever? Or will their love turn Lani into a pumpkin at the stroke of midnight?

***

He was fresh out of new tactics and had no clue how to get her to let down her guard. Plus he had a very strong feeling that he'd pushed her as far as she would go for now. This was looking to be an extended campaign. He didn't like that, but if it was the only way to finally reach her, so be it. "I'll be seeing you in the library—where you will no longer scuttle away every time I get near you."

A hint of the old humor flashed in her eyes. "I never scuttle."

"Scamper? Dart? Dash?"

"Stop it." Her mouth twitched. A good sign, he told himself. "Promise me you won't run off the next time we meet."

The spark of humor winked out. "I just don't like this."

"You've already said that. I'm going to show you there's nothing to be afraid of. Do we have an understanding?"

"Oh, Max..."

"Say yes."

And finally, she gave in and said the words he needed to hear. "Yes. I'll, um, look forward to seeing you."

He didn't believe her. How could he believe her when she sounded so grim, when that mouth he wanted beneath his own was twisted with resignation? He didn't believe her, and he almost wished he could give her what she said she wanted, let her go, say goodbye. He almost wished he could *not* care.

But he'd had so many years of not caring. Years and years when he'd told himself that not caring was for the best.

And then the small, dark-haired woman in front of him changed everything.

***

Enjoy this sneak peek from Christine Rimmer's
THE PRINCE'S CINDERELLA BRIDE,
the latest installment in her Harlequin® Special Edition
miniseries **THE BRAVO ROYALES,** *on sale May 2014!*